D1474951

Dedalus European Classics

The Devil In Love
Jacques Cazotte

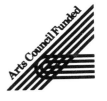

Arts Council Funded

Translated from the French
by
Judith Landry

The Devil in Love

JACQUES CAZOTTE

With an Introduction
by
Brian Stableford

Dedalus

Published in the UK by
Dedalus Ltd,
Langford Lodge, St Judith's Lane,
Sawtry, Cambs, PE17 5XE

ISBN 0 946626 73 1

Publishing History
First published France 1772
Judith Landry's English translation 1991

Printed in England by
Billing & Sons Limited,
Hylton Road, Worcester, WR2 5JU

Typeset by
'Wideyed'
25 Kemerton Road
London SE5 9AP

Judith Landry and the editors of the
Dedalus European Classics Series would like to express their
gratitude to Georgette Illes for her invaluable help in producing
The Devil in Love.

DEDALUS EUROPE 1992

At the end of 1992 the 12 Member States of the EEC will inaugurate an open market which Dedalus is celebrating with a major programme of new translations from the 8 languages of the EEC into English. The new translations will reflect the whole range of Dedalus's publishing programme; classics, literary fantasy and contemporary fiction.

Titles so far selected are:

From French

The Devil in Love - Jacques Cazotte
Trilby and Smarra - Charles Nodier
Angels of Perversity - Remy de Gourmont
Calvary - Octave Mirbeau
The Dedalus Book of French Fantasy - Editor Christine Donougher

From German

The Angel of The West Window - Gustav Meyrink
The Green Face - Gustav Meyrink
The Architect of Ruins - Herbert Rosendorfer
The Dedalus Book of German Fantasy - editor Mike Mitchell

From Italian

Senso (and other stories) - Camillo Boito
One, Nobody and One Hundred Thousand - Luigi Pirandello

From Dutch

The Chronicle of Petty Souls - Louis Couperus
The Dedalus Book of Dutch Fantasy - Editor Richard Huijing

From Dutch/French

The Dedalus Book of Belgian Fantasy - Editor Richard Huijing

From Portuguese

The Mandarin - Eca del Querios
The Relic - Eca del Queiros

From Danish

The Black Cauldron - William Heinesen

From Greek

The History of a Vendetta - Yorgi Yatramanolakis

From Spanish

The Dedalus Book of Spanish Fantasy

Further titles will shortly be announced.

THE TRANSLATOR

Judith Landry was educated at Somerville College, Oxford where she obtained a first class honours degree in French and Italian. She combines a career as a translator of works of fiction, art and architecture with part-time teaching at the Courtauld Institute, London. Her translations include *The House by The Medlar Tree*, by Giovanni Verga and *Dino Buzatti's Short Stories*. Her current projects include a new translation of Luigi Pirandello's *One, Nobody and One Hundred Thousand* as part of the Dedalus Europe 1992 Programme.

THE EDITOR

Brian Stableford was born in Shipley, Yorkshire in 1948 and studied Biology at the University of York, before doing a D.Phil in Sociology. He is one of the UK's leading writers of science fiction and fantastic fiction and his recent novels include *The Empire of Fear* and *The Werewolves of London*. His non-fiction books include *The Sociology of Science Fiction* and *Scientific Romance in Britain 1890 - 1950*.

He has edited several books for Dedalus including *Tales of The Wandering Jew* and *The Dedalus Book of British Fantasy; the 19th c* and the forthcoming *The Dedalus Book of Femmes Fatales*.

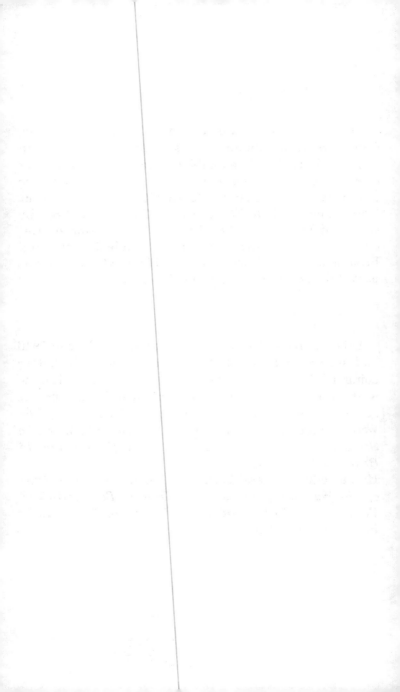

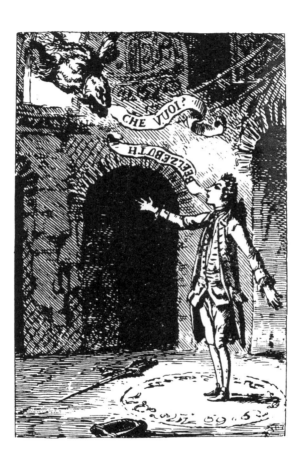

INTRODUCTION
by
Brian Stableford

Jacques Cazotte was born in Dijon in 1719 and educated at the local Jesuit College. There he was extensively schooled in the ancient and modern languages, in order to prepare him for a career in foreign affairs. He subsequently studied law, qualifying in 1740, and shortly after went to Paris in order to enter the Marine Department of the civil service. He was then required by the Admiralty to spend a further two years studying marine law in Paris.

While he was pursuing these further studies Cazotte became a member of one of the capital's many literary salons and produced his earliest literary works, *La patte du chat* (1741) and *Les mille et une fadaises* (1742; tr. as A Thousand and One Follies). Once he had taken up his official duties, however, he found himself fully occupied. He held various posts on shore and aboard ship, and was involved in various naval campaigns against the English during the war of the Austrian Succession.

After being promoted to *écrivain principal* in 1747 Cazotte was posted to the island of Martinique in the Caribbean, where he had an extremely uncomfortable time, dogged by poor health and financial difficulties. He seems to have been very badly treated by his superiors and never received the full remuneration due to him for his services, and in 1752 he was returned to France in order to recover his health and produce a report on the state of the colony. He was drawn once again into the literary life of Paris, producing two ballads and contributing two pamphlets to the controversy that was then raging regarding the alleged inferiority of French operatic music to Italian. Cazotte took up the cause of French music, most notably in a vituperative reply to a critical pamphlet issued by Rousseau.

Cazotte returned to Martinique in 1754 but fared no better than before; his health deteriorated again and the hostility of his superiors was renewed. His awkward situation was further complicated by the outbreak of the Seven Years' War, during which the British tried unsuccessfully to capture Martinique. After being partially blinded by scurvy, Cazotte again returned to France in 1759, but was unfortunate enough to attempt to liquidate his assets by handing them over to a Jesuit Mission in exchange for notes of credit payable by the Society in France. These notes turned out to be virtually worthless, because the Mission's credit was already over-extended (though the refusal of the Society to honour them added to the burden of disrepute which eventually led to the suppression of the French Jesuits in 1764).

Cazotte's financial troubles were compounded by the fact that the Admiralty would not offer him an adequate pension following his premature retirement, and he would have been in a parlous state had he not inherited from his brother (who, being a clergyman, had no children) a large house in Pierry, near Epernay. Here Cazotte stayed for the remainder of his life; shortly after taking up residence there he married the daughter of an officer he had known in Martinique, and the couple had three children.

It was while living quietly at Pierry, at some

distance from but not completely out of touch with the literary world of Paris, that Cazotte wrote his most considerable works, he developed the substance of one of his ballads into the longest of his works *Ollivier* (1763), a burlesque of the chivalric romances which had flattered and delighted the feudal barons of Medieval France, and which remained popular in spite of critical scorn. This was followed in 1767 by a comic novel, *Le Lord impromptu* (tr. as *His most Unlooked for Lordship)* and in 1772 (though it may have been written as many as eight years earlier) by much his most famous work, *Le Diable amoreux* (tr. as *The Devil in Love* and *Biondetta*; or, *The Enamoured Spirit*).

In addition to these three long works Cazotte produced numerous minor pieces, of which several are of some note. *La Nouvelle Raméide* (1766) is a curious 'sequel' to a eulogistic poem issued in the same year by Jean François Rameau, the nephew of the famous composer whose eccentricities were later to be immortalised by Diderot in *Le neveu de Rameau* (written1761; published 1823; tr. as *Rameau's Nephew*). In the same period he dabbled in the production of fables, after the fashion of La Fontaine; these were later collected in 1788, along with various other items, including 'La belle par accident', a Quixotic fairy tale in the same vein as his earliest publications, and 'Rachel' (1788), a new version of a Spanish legend. Cazotte's last major work was a series of oriental tales - some, but not all based in authentic Arabian folklore - issued as a *Continuation des mille et une nuits* (1788-89) tr. as *Arabian Tales*).

Cazotte's interest in the fantastic and the occult, exhibited in almost all his literary works, extended in the latter part of his life to a close involvement with the Martinists, an illuminist sect claiming affiliation to the Rosicrucian Order and Weishaupt's Bavarian Illuminati.

The founder of the sect, Martinez de Pasqualis, had established a series of quasi-masonic lodges in various French cities during the 1760s; after his death in 1768 he was succeeded by the self-styled Saint-Martin, whose close associate Madame la Croix became a member of Cazotte's household, collaborating with him in séances and other occult experiments (somewhat to the discomfort of Mme. Cazotte). It is not clear exactly when Cazotte was initiated into the order, but the occult apparatus of *Le Diable amoureux* is certainly not taken seriously, and it is not until the oriental tales written in the late 1780s that the inspiration of the Martinist ideas becomes obvious in his work.

Cazotte did not remain within the Martinist fold for long; he broke with Saint-Martin in 1789 because the latter favoured the revolutionaries while Cazotte himself remained steadfastly loyal to the king. In fact, Cazotte's loyalty went so far as to encourage him to draw up plans for a hypothetical counter-revolution, which he laid out in letters to an old friend who was an assistant to Laporte, the controller of the Civil List. When Laporte was arrested and his papers seized these letters fell into the hands of the revolutionaries and Cazotte was promptly arrested, along with his daughter Elisabeth. They were imprisoned in the Abbaye Saint-Germain-des Prés, and though they survived a massacre mounted by the Marseillais Cazotte was brought before a revolutionary tribunal, condemned and guillotined in September 1792.

Cazotte's literary work exemplifies many of the popular literary fashions of his day. All of it was written to amuse, and the greater part of it is tongue-in-cheek. Although he was presumably grateful for the money earned by *Le Diable amoureux* and the *Oriental tales* there was never any sign of burgeoning professionalism in his career; he remained an *amateur* throughout. He did not lay claim to any considerable talent or artistry, and most of his critics have agreed with him. Even *Le Diable amoureux*, which is universally considered to be his masterpiece, is something of a curate's egg, brilliant in some respects but distinctly ham-fisted in others. Appropriate assessment of the work is not helped by the fact that (according to Cazotte) the extant text is only half the work which he originally planned, and perhaps wrote, and that its ending had to be rewritten because the first version was deemed unsatisfactory by its readers.

In spite of these reservations, however, it must be asserted that Cazotte is a key figure in the development of modern fantastic fiction, and one of the most important of its founding fathers. He was active in an age when the fantastic materials of oral tradition were first being exploited by *littérateurs*, not in a purely imitative fashion but in an exploratory spirit. He was one of the pioneers who demonstrated that ideas of the supernatural which were incapable of sustaining real belief (his conversion to Martinism cannot be seen as a redemption of the notions deployed in his fiction) became in consequence *more* useful to the writer of amusing, satirical and moralistic fictions. *Le Diable amoureux* is by far his most important work because it proved, in a particularly audacious fashion, that literary dealings with a metaphorical devil can offer a commentary on the tribulations of temptation far more pointed than any pious sermon.

Cazotte's earliest stories reflect the fashionability in early eighteenth century France of the remade folktale. Though Charles Perrault had cautiously issued his collection of *Contes de ma mère Loye* (1697 tr. as *Tales of Mother Goose* and many other titles) under his son's name in order to protect his own reputation for serious work the book took the *salons* of Paris by storm, and inspired dozens of further collections of *contes de fées*, many of them written by aristocratic ladies or clergymen.

Perrault's stories had all been based on traditional tales, reshaped to sustain the moral lessons which were scrupulously appended to them, but those who followed in his footsteps made little or no distinction between original and borrowed materials. Within a few years the fairies were popping up in heavily ironic tales of the contemporary French court, adding an element of burlesque which excused but did not blunt the cutting edge of the satire.

The licence which the deployment of fairies gave to writers was by no means confined to satire. The presence of such elements with a story also defused charges of indecency. Galland's translation of the classic anthology of Arabian folktales, the *Mille et une Nuits* (1704 - 1717) introduced Oriental elements into the genre, and also gave a healthy boost to its eroticism. The satirical irony of the newly-composed tales lent itself very readily to fusion with flirtatiously licentious material, and the importation of such material did no harm at all to the popularity of such tales in the Parisian *salons*. Everyone agreed - was it not entirely obvious? - that such tales were mere literary confections, and that they should in consequence be allowed a latitude which was not yet to be extended to more seriously-inclined work. (But 'everyone', of course, does not include the English, whose own extrapolations of the fairy tale were much more modest in every respect).

Inevitably, the Orientalized fairy tale was itself satirized, most notably by Antoine Hamilton (though Hamilton's most famous work, and the only one to be translated into English - *Les Quatre Facardins* (1710 - 15) - remained incomplete), and it is not suprising that Cazotte, writing in the early 1740s, should have moved rapidly from the light-hearted but relatively straight *La Patte du Chat* to the chaotic absurdity of *Les mille et une fadaises*.

The former tale, openly imitative of Thomas Gueullette's pastiches of Galland, describes the amazing adventures of the long-nosed Amadil, exiled from the country of Zimzim for treading on the paw of the queen's favourite cat (which turns out, in the end, to be an evil magician in disguise). The latter establishes its credentials by posing as a tale concocted by an abbé as a cure for the insomnia of two bored ladies of leisure. Its opening parodies the tale of the sleeping beauty, though the multiply hunchbacked evil fairy is somewhat inconvenienced in delivering her curse by virtue of getting stuck in the chimney; and its penultimate sequence parodies the most celebrated of the licentious fairy tales, *Le Sopha* (1740) by Crébillon fils, in featuring a room entirely furnished by people magically transformed into appropriate pieces of furniture. The middle of the story is interrupted by an entirely irrelevant account of the adventures of a knight from the moon who has descended to earth by filling his head with ideas, thus rendering himself vulnerable to the force of gravity which is impotent to affect his light-minded fellow lunarians.

It is interesting to contrast these early tales, which are intentionally slapdash, with *'La belle par accident'*, a story of the same type first published nearly half a century afterwards. Here the hero Kallibad is an avatar of Don Quixote, deluded by overindulgence in the delights of the fantastic fiction into an inability to separate fact from fancy, but Cazotte is far more forgiving than Cervantes was and is careful to excuse and endorse a moderate level of affection for fantasy.

Ollivier attempts to do for the chivalric romance what *La patte du chat* does for the fairy tale, but in pursuit of propriety it extends to a much greater length. Cazotte seems not to have been entirely comfortable with a project of this magnitude, probably because he was used to making up his plots as he went along, and the confused nature of the story is more a lack of organization than calculated satire. The four subplots are untidily entwined, and the eventual *dénouement* is both anti-climatic and incomplete. If, as is sometimes alleged, the model of the story is Ariosto's *Orlando Furioso*, the imitation is very pale indeed.

Just as he returned to the *conte de fées* in the latter part of of his career, so Cazotte returned to the chivalric romance, with the much shorter *'L'Honneur perdu et recouvré'* (published 1788). The irony in this later tale is so muted as to be almost imperceptible, and it passed for a genuine example of the species with the ironic result that it became popular with a wider readership than most of the author's other works.

Le Lord impromptu is a more interesting experiment than *Ollivier*, although it stands almost alone in Cazotte's *oeuvre* in having no supernatural elements. It masquerades as a translation from the English and its models are to be found among the less earnest of early English novels - it is closest in spirit to Fielding's parodies of Richardson, especially *Joseph Andrews* (1842). Its hero, Richard O'Berthon, is raised as a gentleman and a scholar, but loses his income and is forced to seek employment as a servant. Thus misplaced within the class structure (a fate which he shares, of course, with the heroes and heroines of countless English domestic melodramas) he is inevitably drawn to commit the cardinal sin of falling in love with the daughter of the house in which he is employed. In the wake of a tragic misunderstanding he is forced to flee the vengeance of his employer, and spends the greater part of the novel disguised as a girl, under the protection of the enigmatic and resourceful Captain Sentry (who ultimately turns out to be his mother in male disguise).

The outsider's view of English manners and the clichés of English popular fiction which is presented in *Le Lord impromptu* is understandably jaundiced, and it is not entirely suprising that in spite of its setting and subject-matter the novel was not translated into English until 1927. Few English commentators have had a kind word to say about the work, but it certainly demonstrates that Cazotte was not a one-book writer and although the story is utterly incredible it is the most coherently-plotted of all his works.

THE DEVIL IN LOVE

Le Diable amoureux is by far the most original of Cazotte's works, taking fantastic fiction into fields which were then entirely fresh. The idea of erotic temptation was by no means new, (the danger posed by demonic *succubi* having been included in the preaching of churchmen for several centuries,) but the idea that myth arose from and remained connected with erotic dreams was.

Although there is a point in *Le Diable amoureux* when Alvaro wonders whether his entire adventure has been delusory there cannot possibly be any suggestion that it could all have been the dream of a single night.

Although many of Alvaro's adventures are written off as purely subjective experiences there is no doubt that Biondetta is real and that her attendance upon the hero extends over a long period.

Cazotte was later to say that the work as originally envisaged had two parts, the first describing Alvaro's seduction and the second following his subsequent career as the devil's minion. He explained the non-publication of the second part (which, if it ever existed, has been lost) by saying that it was too dark to be welcomed by an audience in search of amusement and distraction. The removal of the second part was initially compounded by a softening of the first part; in the version presented in the first edition Biondetta does not complete her seduction but gives away her true nature by her calmness in the face of the storm, and is commanded to vanish - which she does, after briefly showing her true form for a second time. This abrupt conclusion proved unsatisfactory, however, and so Cazotte added (or perhaps restored) the episode of the farmhouse, in which Alvaro finally yields to temptation.

The rewritten ending certainly provides a more interesting climax, but it also has the effect of significantly compromising the moralizing of the story. Alvaro's mother, whose memory and image have functioned throughout the plot as a metaphorical guardian angel protecting Alvaro against Biondetta's wiles is again invoked as a saviour, but it is not at all clear that Alvaro's salvation from the consequences of his weakness is appropriate.

Had Cazotte stuck to his original plan, and let Alvaro become a living servant of the devil, his story would appear very different to the modern reader; it would be an important prototype of Gothic fantasy. Indeed, insofar as *Le Diable amoureux* was influential upon the work of other writers it seems to have nourished Gothic writers far more than writers in a lighter vein. Critics are uncertain as to whether it should be counted among the influences of Matthew Gregory Lewis's gaudy tale of horror *The Monk* (1796), which features erotic temptation in a more lurid vein, but it seems not unlikely, given the fact that Lewis was sufficiently familiar with French work of the period to write his own conclusion to Hamilton's *Four Facardins* for an English edition. There is no doubt, though, that Cazotte was read and much admired by the most important writers of terror tales, E. T. A. Hoffman and Ludwig Tieck. In the form in which *Le Diable amoureux* has actually been handed down, however, it is more closely related to a kind of fantasy which was to become much more openly sceptical of received ideas of good and evil.

In the truncated tale with the revised ending Biondetta

does the hero no lasting harm at all, and his romantic adventure with her might thus be counted (although this was not the author's intention) entirely to his credit. For this reason, *Le Diable amoureux* stands at the head of a series of daringly sceptical works which gradually muster more and more sympathy for the supposed agents of evil; it has clear thematic links with Théophile Gautier's *'La morte amoureuse'* (1836; tr. as *'The Dead Leman'* and *'Clarimonde'*), whose title may well carry a deliberate echo, and with such stories by Anatole France as *'Leslie Wood'* (1892) and *La révolte des anges* (1914; tr. as *Revolt of the Angels*). In these stories the pleasure-denying morality of the church is severely questioned, and ultimately condemned, and though that was not Cazotte's aim it is easy enough to believe that - like Milton, according to Blake - he was 'of the devil's party without knowing it'. The modern reader who follows Alvaro's affair with the ever obliging Biondetta can hardly help but find her charming even while refusing to be duped by the false explanation of her nature which she gives.

Ironically, if the imagery of Cazotte's tale lent inspiration to those who wanted to argue that the devil was not as black as the church painted him, it also offered some inspiration for those who wanted to believe that all seductive women had a little of the devil in them. Thus Baudelaire sometimes invoked Cazotte while lamenting his unhappy relationships with the opposite sex, and there is an echo of *Le Diable amoureux* in Barbey d' Aurevilly's collection *Les Diaboliques* (1874; tr. as *Weird Women* and *The She - Devils*).

It has to be admitted that the importance of Cazotte's tale is largely historical; so many tales of diabolical bargain have been published since 1772 that it cannot help but seem pale and hesitant by comparison with the best of them. But it remains very readable, and holds its essential fascination for anyone who can read it with an awareness of its context. It is astonishing that it has been out of print in the English language for more than half a century (and had been out of print before that for nearly a hundred years).

It would be premature to conclude this introduction without mentioning an episode which has probably contributed more to Cazotte's posthumous celebrity than anything which he actually did or wrote, and that is the prophecy which he is said to have issued early in 1788. This became famous enough to seem appropriate as the very first matter to come under consideration the last time anyone had the privilege of introducing one of Cazotte's books to an English audience (Storm Jameson, in the 1927 edition of *A Thousand and One Follies* and *His Most Unlooked-For Lordship*).

According to the story, Cazotte, whose reputation as a Martinist mystic was by then secure, told a sceptical gathering of the cream of the French intelligentsia - including the most celebrated of the philosophers of progress, the Marquis de Condorcet - exactly what fates would befall them in the coming years. Inevitably, so the story goes, these great men of the Age of Reason declined to believe that so many of them would die on the scaffold or in prison; nor would they credit Cazotte's further insistence that the king and queen would be included among the victims of the coming Terror.

This prophecy has one point in common with all great

prophecies - which is to say that there is no record of it whatsoever in advance of the events which it supposedly foretold. Jean-François de La Harpe, who claimed to have been present, left a very elaborate account of it in his papers, but this was not published until 1806, by which time La Harpe was dead and could not be questioned about it. One suspects, of course, that the gifts of hindsight might conceivably have been brought to the assistance of La Harpe's memory when he wrote his account, and there is written evidence to supplement the conviction born of common sense, that La Harpe intended his account as an allegory rather than a memoir (it was probably intended to dramatize the inconceivability, in 1788, of his post-revolution conversion from free thought to Catholicism). Needless to say, though, the prophecy was very widely quoted, and has frequently been advanced as good evidence of the indubitable superhuman powers of the illuminati and all who follow in their footsteps.

What the story of the supposed prophecy actually tells us, of course, is that the love-affair which the nobility of eighteenth century France had with the substance of fantasy was not quite the superficial dalliance that it seemed. The comedy and the burlesque, as always, masked real anxieties and touched upon deep - seated doubts. Even the greatest figures of the Enlightenment succumbed to the temptation to involve themselves with such writings - not only Diderot but also Voltaire (with whom Cazotte was acquainted and of whom he disapproved) - and proved by their example that even the most frothy literary confections could be fully-loaded with caustic sarcasm.

Jacques Cazotte was not in the same intellectual league

as Diderot and Voltaire, and this shows in the comparison of their various fantastic fictions as well as in the fact that he eventually plumped for Mysticism instead of Reason, but he was a player of the same great game, which should by no means be written off as a trivial and insignificant amusement of no relevance to more serious affairs. As J. R. R. Tolkien has reminded us, he whose imagination is too closely bound by a straitjacket of actuality cannot properly see where the bounds of Reason lie, and what the implications of Reason truly are. Unless we can understand nonsense we cannot clearly see sense; that is why works like *Le Diable amoureux* are important, not only in the history of literature, but in the furnishing of intelligent minds.

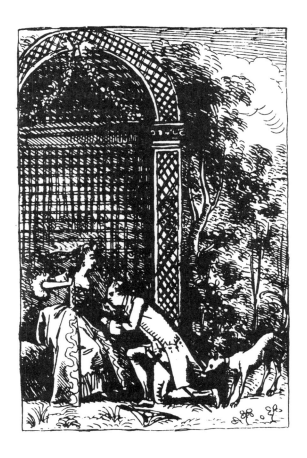

THE DEVIL IN LOVE

At the age of twenty-five I was a captain in the king's guard at Naples; we kept our own company much of the time, and lived after the manner of young men, that is, gaming and womanising, as long as our purses could bear it; and we would philosophize in our quarters when we no longer had any other resources.

One evening, after we had exhausted ourselves through all manner of argument around a very small bottle of Cyprus wine and a few dried chestnuts, conversation turned to the Cabbala and cabbalists.

One of our number claimed that it was a true science, whose workings were certainties; four of the youngest amongst us objected that it was a mass of absurdities, a source of knavery, fit to dupe the credulous and to amuse children.

The oldest amongst us, Flemish by origin, was smoking his pipe with an absent air and saying nothing. I was struck by his cool, withdrawn demeanour, in such contrast with the prevailing deafening racket, and this prevented me from taking part in a conversation that was too ill-ordered to hold any interest for me.

We were in the pipe-smoker's room; the hour was becoming late; the crowd broke up and we remained alone, the older man and me.

He continued to smoke unperturbed; I continued sitting there, my elbows on the table, without saying a word. At last my man broke the silence.

"Young man," he said, "you have just been listening to a lot of sound and fury; why did you retire from the mêlèe?"

"Because," I replied, I prefer to keep silent rather than to approve or censure things I know nothing of. I do not even know what the word Cabbala means."

"It has several meanings," he told me; "but we are not concerned with them, we are concerned with the thing itself. Do you believe in the possible existence of a science which teaches the transformation of metals and the bringing of spirits under our control?"

"I know nothing of spirits, beginning with my own, except that I am sure of its existence. As for metals, I know the value of a carlino at gaming, at the inn and elsewhere, but I cannot state or deny anything as to the essence of either spirit or metal, or as to the modifications and processes of which they are susceptible."

"My young comrade, I like your ignorance; it is as good as others' learning; at least you are not misguided, and if you are not educated, you are capable of becoming so. I like your disposition, the frankness of your character, your uprightness of spirit; I know a little more than the common ruck of mortals; swear the greatest discretion on your word of honour, promise me to conduct yourself with prudence, and you shall be my pupil."

"My dear Soberano, your invitation is most acceptable. Curiosity is my besetting passion. I may admit to you that by nature I have little eagerness for our ordinary body of knowledge; it has always seemed to me too limited, and I had already divined this exalted sphere to which you would help me to ascend. Tell me, what is the first key to the science of which you speak? Judging by what our comrades were saying in their debate, it is the spirits themselves who teach us; can one ally oneself with them?"

"You have said the word, Alvaro; one would learn nothing on one's own; and as to the feasibility of our liaisons, I shall give you incontrovertible proof of it."

As he was finishing these words, he was also finishing his pipe; he knocked three times to empty out the little remaining ash, put it down near me on the table. He raised his voice: "Calderon," said he, "come and get my pipe, light it and bring it back to me." He had hardly formulated his order than I saw the pipe disappear; and, before I could consider the means, or enquire as to the nature of the mysterious Calderon who was the recipient of his command, the lit pipe was back again, and my interlocutor had resumed his occupation.

He continued thus for some time, less to savour the tobacco than to bask in the surprise he had engendered; then, rising, he said: "I am on duty at dawn, I must get some sleep. You should go back to bed too; be prudent; we shall see each other again."

I withdrew full of curiosity and athirst for new ideas, promising myself my fill of them soon with the help of Soberano. I saw him the next day and during those that followed; this passion filled me entirely; I became his shadow.

I asked him a thousand questions; he avoided some and answered others, in the tone of an oracle. Finally, I pressed him as to the religion of his fellows. "It is natural religion," he replied. We entered into a few details; all this tallied with my intentions rather than my principles; but I wanted to attain my goal and could not vex him.

"You give the spirits orders," I said to him; "I want to be in contact with them, as you are. That is my dearest wish."

"You are impatient, comrade, you have not been through your period of trial; you have fulfilled none of the conditions through which one may approach this sublime category with impunity..."

"Will it take long?"

"Two years, perhaps..."

"Then I shall abandon the whole thing," I cried; "I would die of impatience in the meanwhile. You are cruel, Soberano. You cannot imagine the intensity of the desire you have awakened in me; it is all-consuming..."

"Young man, I credited you with more prudence; you make me tremble for yourself and me. What! Would you venture to call up spirits without any of the necessary preparation?"

"Well? What could happen to me?"

"I am not saying that anything harmful would necessarily befall you; if they have power over us, it is given to them by our own weakness, our faintheartedness. Essentially, we are born to command them..."

"Oh, I shall surely command!"

"Yes, you are mettlesome indeed; but what if you lose your head, if they suddenly alarm you?"

"If it is simply a matter of not fearing them, I shall defy them to alarm me."

"What! If you saw the Devil himself?"

"I'd pull his devilish ears for him!"

"Bravo. If you are so sure of yourself, you can take the plunge and I promise you my assistance. Next Friday, I invite you to dine with two of our initiates, and we shall embark upon our adventure."

It was only Tuesday; no gallant assignation had ever been awaited with such eagerness. At last the moment arrived; I met two unprepossessing men in Soberano's rooms and we dined. The conversation touched upon neutral matters.

After dinner, a walk in the direction of Portici was suggested. Upon our arrival, the remains of those most august monuments, now crumbling, shattered, scattered, bramble-ridden, aroused unaccustomed ideas in me. "Here," said I , "we see the power of time over the pride and industry of men." We proceeded through the ruins and at last, more or less groping our way through the debris, we arrived at a place whose darkness was untouched by any external light.

My comrade was leading me by the arm; he stopped walking, and I stood still. Then one of the company lit a candle. The place was illuminated, albeit feebly, and I saw that we were under a fairly well-preserved vault, some twenty feet high, and with four exits.

Utter silence was observed. Using his cane, my comrade drew a circle around him in the light sand that covered the ground, and emerged from it after tracing several characters. "Enter this pentacle, amigo," said he, "and leave it only on good authority..."

"Explain yourself more clearly: on what authority should I leave it?"

"You may leave it when you are in a position of command; but until that time, should fear cause you to take a false step, you would be running the gravest risk."

Then he gave me a short, insistent formula for the calling up of spirits, mingled with a few words I shall never forget.

"Pronounce the spell firmly," he told me, "and then call Beelzebub clearly three times, and above all do not forget what you promised to do."

I remembered that I had boasted that I would pull the devil's ears. "I shall keep my word," I told him, not wishing to appear ignominious by failing to take up the challenge.

"We wish you much success," he said; "when you have finished, kindly let us know. You are standing directly opposite the door through which you must leave in order to rejoin our company." They withdrew.

Never had braggart landed himself in tighter corner. I was on the point of calling them back; but it would have been too demeaning, as well as tantamount to abandoning all my hopes. I stood firm, and pondered for a moment. They are trying to frighten me, I thought; they want to see if I am a coward. Those who are testing me are but two steps away and, after I have spoken the spell, I must be prepared for them to make some attempt to scare me. I must stand fast; I must have the last laugh.

This deliberation was quite short, although somewhat disturbed by the hooting of the owls nesting in the surrounding trees, and indeed within my cave itself.

Slightly reassured by my reflections, I crouched down and dug in my heels; I pronounced the formula in a clear, unwavering voice; and, rising to a crescendo, three times, in staccato fashion, I called *Beelzebub*.

A frisson ran through my veins, and my hair bristled on my head. Hardly had I finished, than a window opened up in front of me, at the top of the vault: a flood of light more dazzling than that of day poured in through the opening; a camel's head, as hideous in size as in shape, appeared at the window; the ears in particular were disproportionately large. The odious phantom opened its muzzle and, in tones assorting with the rest of the apparition, answered me: "Che vuoi?" (What is it you wish?)

I was quite unequal to the situation; I do not know what bolstered my courage and prevented me from falling into a faint at that sight and at the even more dreadful sound which echoed in my ears.

I felt the need to rally my forces; a cold sweat was threatening to dissipate them; I steadied myself. The soul must indeed be many-mansioned and prodigiously resilient; a throng of feelings, ideas and reflections spoke to my heart and passed through my mind simultaneously.

The revolution was achieved, I had mastered my terror, I fixed the spectre boldly.

"What do you mean, oh brazen one, by appearing in this hideous guise?"

The phantom hesitated for a moment:

"You summoned me," it said in a quieter tone.

"Does the slave," I queried, "try to frighten his master? If you come here to receive my orders, you should adopt a fitting shape and a submissive tone."

"Master," the phantom asked me, "in what form should I present myself to be agreeable to you? "

The first idea that came into my head being that of a dog, "Come in the form of a spaniel," I told him. Hardly had I given the order, than the fearful camel lengthened its neck by sixteen feet, lowered its head right down into the middle of the room, and spewed up a white spaniel with soft silky hair and ears down to the ground.

The window had shut again, the camel had disappeared, and all that remained under the dimly-lit vault was the dog, and me.

He was going round the circle, wagging his tail, and gambolling.

"Master," he addressed me, "I would lick the tips of your

feet, but the impassible circle around you prevents my doing so."

My confidence had soared to the point of audacity: I left the circle, I held out my foot, the dog licked it; I made a gesture to pull its ears, it rolled over on to its back as though to ask forgiveness; I saw that it was a little bitch.

"Get up," I told it; "I forgive you; as you see, I have company; the other gentlemen are waiting some way off; their stroll has probably made them thirsty, I wish to give them a cold collation; we need fruit, preserves, ice cream, Greek wine; let there be no misunderstanding: the room must be lit and decorated in a modest but seemly fashion. Towards the end of the meal, you will enter as a virtuoso of great talent, carrying a harp; I shall let you know when to appear. Be careful to play your part well, put expression into your song, and decency and restraint into your bearing..."

"I shall obey, master, but under what condition?"

"Upon that of obeying, slave. Obey, without a word, or else..."

"You do not know me, master, or you would treat me less harshly: I might perhaps stipulate one sole condition: that I succeed in disarming you."

The dog had scarcely finished than, turning on my heel, I saw my orders executed more promptly than a scene being changed at the Opera. The walls of the vault, previously black, dank and moss-covered, took on a gentle hue, a pleasing form: we were now in a hall of mottled marble, roofed with a semi-circular arch supported by columns. Eight crystal girandoles, each with three candles, cast a bright even light.

One moment afterwards, the table and sideboard were

in place and were loaded with all the trimmings for our feast; the fruits and preserves were of the rarest and most savorous, and beautiful to behold. The porcelain of the serving plates and on the sideboard was from Japan. The little bitch rushed all about the room, performing a thousand curvets around me as though to hasten the process, and asked me whether I was satisfied.

"Excellent, Biondetta," I told her; "take a livery and go and tell the other gentlemen that I am awaiting them, and that they are served."

Hardly had I turned my gaze away for a moment, than I saw a smartly attired page wearing my livery, holding a lighted candelabra; shortly afterwards he returned, leading my companions, the Fleming and his two friends. Though prepared by the page's arrival and announcement for something out of the ordinary, they were nonetheless unprepared for the change that had been wrought upon the place where they had left me. If I had not been occupied by other thoughts, I would have been more than amused at their surprise; it was expressed by cries of amazement and by their expressions and their attitudes.

"Gentlemen," I said to them, "you have travelled a long way on my behalf, and we still have to return to Naples: I thought that you might not be displeased by this little banquet, and that you would excuse the absence of choice and quantity in consideration of the extempore nature of the occasion."

My cool demeanour disconcerted them even more than the change of scene and the sight of the elegant collation to which they found themselves bidden. I noticed this and, determined speedily to conclude an adventure of which I was inwardly mistrustful, I resolved to gain as much advantage from it as possible, if necessary even by exaggerating the gaiety which lies at the root of my character.

I pressed them to take their places at table; the page drew up the chairs with wonderful promptitude. We took our seats; I had filled the glasses and handed round the fruit; my mouth alone opened and closed to eat and talk, the others' remained agape; nonetheless I pressed them to start upon the fruit; my confidence convinced them. I proposed a toast to the loveliest courtesan in Naples, and we drank to her health. I talked of a new opera, of a recently arrived Roman *improvvisatrice* whose talents were the talk of the court. I held forth upon various pleasing attainments, upon music and sculpture; and I had occasion to have them agree on the beauty of certain marbles embellishing the salon. One bottle was emptied, and replaced by an even better one. The page was everywhere at once, and the service never flagged for an instant. I cast a covert glance in his direction: imagine Cupid decked out as a page; my companions were ogling him in their turn with looks bespeaking mingled surprise, pleasure and disquiet. The monotony of this situation annoyed me; I saw that it was time to break it.

"Biondetto," I said to the page, "signora Fiorentina promised to grant us a moment; go and see if she has arrived yet." Biondetto left the room.

Before my guests had even had time to feel astonishment at the bizarre nature of the message, a door to the salon opened and Fiorentina entered holding her harp; she was attired in a modest, flowing garment, a travelling hat with a flimsy veil over her eyes; she set her harp down beside her, and greeted us with ease and grace:

"Signor don Alvaro," she said, "I was not warned that you had company; I would not have presented myself dressed as I am; these gentlemen must forgive me, I am merely passing through."

She sat down, and we vied in offering her what remained of our little banquet, which she accepted out of pure politeness.

"What, Madame?" I asked her, "you are not staying in Naples? Can we not keep you here?"

"A long-standing engagement forces me to leave, sir; I was kindly received in Venice last carnival-time; I had to promise to return, and I have received advance payment; otherwise, I would not have been able to resist the advantages which the court here offers me, and the hope of earning the approbation of the Neapolitan nobility, whose taste distinguishes it above that of all Italy."

The two Neapolitans bowed to acknowledge their praise, so struck by the scene's verisimilitude that they began rubbing their eyes. I pressed the virtuoso to allow us to hear a sample of her talent. She had a cold, she was tired, she pleaded; she rightly feared that she might sink in our estimation. At last she was persuaded to execute an *obbligato* recitative and a moving little aria which ended the third act of the opera in which she was to make her debut.

She took her harp and began to play; her hands were small, slender and dimpled, at once pink and white, their fingers, oh so slightly rounded at the tips, were fringed with nails whose shape and grace were inconceivable; we were all taken by surprise , and felt ourselves to be at the most delicious concert. As she sang, I realized that a powerful voice does not necessarily have greater soulfulness, greater expressiveness, than a soft one: never had gentle voice stirred more emotion. I was moved to the depths of my being, and almost forgot that I was the creator of the charms which ravished me.

The singer addressed the tender expression of her recitative and song to me. The fire of her gaze pierced through the veil; its sweetness and persistence were indescribable; those eyes were not unknown. At last, fitting together the features as the veil allowed me to glimpse them, I recognized in Fiorentina that rascal Biondetto; but the elegance of her figure was shown to much more striking advantage in the guise of a woman than in the costume of a page.

When the singer had finished, we gave her due applause. I wanted to engage her to execute a lively arietta so that we could admire the diversity of her talents.

"No," she answered; "in my present state of mind I would acquit myself poorly; besides, you must have noticed the effort required to obey you. My voice has been affected by the journey, it is husky. I think you should know that I am leaving tonight. A hired coachman brought me here, I am dependent on him; I beg you to accept my excuses, and to allow me to retire." With these words, she stood up and was about to carry off her harp. I took it from her, accompanied her to the door and rejoined the company.

I had intended to inspire gaiety, and I saw constraint on their faces; I had recourse to the Cyprus wine. I found it delicious, it gave me back my strength, my presence of mind; I drank more deeply and, as the hour was becoming late, I told my page, who had reappeared at his place behind my seat, that he should summon my carriage. Biondetto promptly went out to execute my orders.

"You have a carriage here?" Soberano asked me.

"Yes," I replied, "I gave orders that I should be followed, and I thought that if our party continued into the night, you would not be averse to returning in comfort. Let us drink more wine, we have no need to fear false steps on our return."

My words were scarcely out of my mouth, than the page was back with two well-turned-out attendants, superbly attired in my livery. "Senor Don Alvaro," said Biondetto, "I was unable to have your carriage brought any closer; it awaits you outside the surrounding debris." We arose, Biondetto and the attendants preceding us, and walked towards the carriage.

As we could not walk four abreast between the plinths and broken columns, Soberano, who found himself alone at my side, shook my hand: "You have given us fine entertainment, my friend; you will pay a price for it."

"My friend," I answered, "I am delighted if you enjoyed it; it was my pleasure."

We now arrived at the carriage; here we found two other attendants, a coachman, a postillion, a country carriage all at my command, as comfortable as one could wish. I did the honours and, light of heart, we took the road to Naples.

For a time we kept silent; at last our silence was broken by one of Soberano's friends. "I will not ask you your secret, Alvaro; but you must have reached a very singular agreement; no one has ever been served as you are; and during the forty years I have been at work, I have never obtained a quarter of the favours you have been shown in a single evening. I am talking about your being offered the most sublime vision possible, while our eyes are more often offended than delighted... still, you know your own business; at your age one is too greedy to allow oneself time to reflect, and one is over-hasty in one's enjoyment."

Bernardillo, for such was his name, was taking pleasure in the sound of his own voice, and gave me time to ponder my reply.

"I do not know," I answered him, "how I have managed to bring such distinguished favours upon myself; I sense that they will be short-lived, and my consolation will be that I have shared them with my good friends." It was clear that I was being somewhat guarded, and our conversation ceased.

However, silence led to reflection: I recalled what I had seen and done; I compared the words of Soberano and Bernardillo, and concluded that I had just emerged from the tightest corner into which vain curiosity and temerity had ever lured a young man of my condition.

I was not uneducated: until the age of thirteen I had been raised under the eyes of don Bernardo Maravillas, my father, an irreproachable man of gentle birth, and by dona Mencia, my mother, the most religious and estimable woman in all Estremadura. "Oh mother!" I said to myself. "What would you think of your son if you could see him now? But I shall mend my ways, I give you my word."

Meanwhile the carriage was approaching Naples. I accompanied Soberano's friends back to their homes. He and I returned to our quarters. My elegant carriage somewhat dazzled the guard, but the charms of Biondetto, who was on the box, made an even greater impression on the onlookers.

The page dismissed carriage and servants, took a torch from the attendant's hand and walked through the barracks to lead me to my apartments. My valet, even more astonished than the rest, was trying to question me about the new retinue I had just flaunted. "That will do, Carlo," I told him, going into my room. "I do not need you now; go and rest, I shall speak to you to-morrow."

Wishing to conclude this adventure, I withdrew for a moment to take pause for reflection. I cast my eyes upon the page, while his own were fixed upon the ground; the colour rose to his cheeks under my gaze; his countenance revealed unease and much emotion; at last I took it upon myself to speak.

"Biondetto, you have served me well, indeed, with grace; but as you were paid in advance, I think we are quits."

"Don Alvaro is too noble to believe that he could dismiss me thus..."

"If you have done more than the necessary, if I still owe you something, name your figure; but I do not say that you will be paid forthwith. My current quarterage is quite used up; I owe at the gaming table, at the inn, at the tailor's..."

"This lightness is ill-timed."

"If I drop this jesting, it will be to ask you to retire, for it is late and I must go to bed."

"And you would send me off so uncivilly at this hour? I would never have expected this treatment from a Spanish gentleman. Your friends know that I am here, your soldiers and your servants have seen me and have divined my sex. If I were but a courtesan, you would have some consideration for the proprieties required by my estate;

.viour towards me is insulting; any woman
iiliated by it."
ou elect to become a woman to earn yourself
favours. Well then! To avoid the scandal of your
departure, kindly show yourself due respect and retire
through the keyhole."

"What? Truly, might you suggest, not knowing who I
am...."

"Could I fail to?"

"You do not know, I tell you, you are merely heeding
your preconceptions. But whoever I am, I am at your feet,
with tears in my eyes; I am beseeching you as an inferior.
Temerity greater than your own, excusable perhaps, since
you are its object, has to-day caused me to brave
everything, to sacrifice all, in order to obey you, to
surrender and to follow you. I have allowed the most cruel
passions, the most implacable emotions, to arise, and I am
in danger: my only remaining protection comes from you,
my only safe haven is your room. Would you close it
against me? Shall it be said the a Spanish gentleman has
shown such harshness, such baseness to one who has
sacrificed all for him - a sensitive soul, a defenceless being
lacking all other help - in a word, a person of my sex?"

I drew back as best I could to extricate myself from this
predicament; but she was embracing my knees and
following me on her own. Finally I found myself against
the wall. "Get up," I said to her, "unwittingly you have
just taken me up on my oath. When my mother gave me
my first sword, she made me swear, on its hilt, that I
would serve women all my life, and not displease a single
one. Had she known, then..."

"Whatever the reason, oh cruel one, allow me to remain

44

in your room."

"The unusual nature of the affair, and my desire to conclude this whole bizarre adventure, lead me to agree. Try to dispose yourself so that I may neither see nor hear you; at the first word, at the first movement which might cause me concern, I shall raise my voice to ask you in your turn: *Che vuoi?*"

I turned from her and went to my bed to undress. "Shall I help you?" I was asked. "No, I am a soldier and need no assistance." Whereupon I climbed into bed.

Through the gauze of my curtains I saw the alleged page arranging a threadbare rug he had found in a wardrobe in a corner of my room. He sat down upon it, undressed completely, wrapped himself up in a cloak of mine that had been lying on a chair, turned out the light, and there the scene ended, for the moment; soon to begin again in my bed, where sleep evaded me.

It was as though the portrait of the page were pinned to the ceiling of the bed, and upon its four posters; I saw only him. I tried in vain to link the ravishing object with the idea of the frightful phantom; the first apparition served merely to heighten the charm of the second.

The melodious song which I had heard under the vault, the sound of that ravishing voice, that speech which seemed to come from the heart, still echoed in my own.

Ah Biondetta, I said to myself, if only you were not an imaginary being; if only you were not that hideous dromedary!

But what was I allowing myself to be drawn into? I had triumphed over fear, now let us stamp out a more dangerous emotion. What quarter could I expect? Would not such a being always be the creature of its own origins?

The ardour of those sweet and touching glances was a cruel poison. That perfectly formed mouth, so red, so fresh and apparently so innocent, opened only to utter deceits. That heart, if heart it were, would warm only for betrayal.

While I was giving myself over to reflections occasioned by the various impulses with which I was seized, the moon, which had climbed to the height of the hemisphere in a cloudless sky, was darting its rays into my chamber through three large casements.

I was making prodigious movements in my bed, which was not new; suddenly the wood shattered, and the three boards which supported my mattress fell noisily to the floor.

Biondetta rose, ran towards me and enquired in a tone of alarm: "Don Alvaro, what misfortune has befallen you?"

As I had my eyes upon her, despite my accident, I saw her rise and run towards me; her chemise was that of a page and, as she passed, the moonlight falling upon her thigh seemed to gain in beauty.

Mightily unconcerned at the poor state of my bed, which meant merely that I would sleep a little less comfortably, I was far more unsettled at finding myself enfolded in Biondetta's arms.

"I am not hurt," I said, "please go away; you are walking on the tiles barefooted, you will catch cold, please go away..."

"But you are not comfortable..."

"No, and you are the cause; now go away or, since you insist on sleeping in my apartments and near me, I shall order you to go and sleep in the spider's web at the corner of my room." She did not wait for me to finish the threat and went to lie down on her rug, sobbing softly.

46

The night was drawing to an end and exhaustion, gaining the upper hand, procured me a few moments of repose. I did not awaken again till daybreak. The direction taken by my waking gaze is easily divined. I sought my page.

He was seated on a little stool, already dressed save for his doublet; he had unloosed his hair, which reached the ground, covering his back and shoulders and indeed his face with flowing natural curls.

For want of any other means, he was combing his hair with his fingers. Never did ivory comb wander through a denser forest of ash blond hair, whose fineness equalled all its other perfections; a slight movement of mine having announced my awakening, she drew aside the curls which half hid her face. Imagine a spring dawn rising from the mists of the morning, with all its dew, its freshness and its scents.

"Biondetta," I told her, "take a comb; there are several in the drawer of that desk." She obeyed and soon, with the help of a ribbon, her hair was drawn up on her head with as much skill as elegance. She took her doublet, put the finishing touches to her attire and sat down again on her seat with a timid, abashed, apprehensive air which suddenly aroused my keen compassion.

If, I told myself, I have to witness a thousand such tableaux during the day, each more piquant than the last, I shall certainly not be able to keep my resolve; let us hasten the dénouement, if that be possible.

"Day is come, Biondetta," I said to her, "appearances have been kept up and you can now leave the room without any danger of ridicule."

"By now," she answered, "I am beyond such fears; but

your interest, and mine also, inspires in me a fear more serious by far: it does not allow us to part."

"Will you explain yourself?"

"I am about to do so, Alvaro. Your youth, your temerity blind you to the perils we have woven around us. The moment I saw you beneath the vault, your heroic bearing in the face of the most hideous apparition determined my inclinations. I told myself that if, to attain happiness, I must be united with a mortal, then the time had come, I would take on bodily form. Here was a hero worthy of me. No matter that his despicable rivals might be outraged and no matter that I might find myself exposed to their resentment and vengeance; loved by Alvaro, united with Alvaro, and nature itself will be in our thrall. You knew what was to be.

Envy, jealousy and spite threaten the cruellest of punishments for beings of my kind, degraded as they are by their choice; and you alone can shield me from them. It is barely daybreak, and already the informers are out to denounce you, as a necromancer, to a certain court. In an hour..."

"Stop," I shouted, putting my clenched fists over my eyes, "you are a very mistress of deceit. You speak of love, you present its image, but you poison the very idea; I forbid you to speak of it. Let me calm myself sufficiently, if I can, to become capable of taking a decision.

If I must fall into the hands of the court, then I shall not waver between you and it; but if you help me out of this predicament, what will I be committing myself to? Will I be able to leave you, should I so desire? I order you to answer me clearly and precisely."

"To leave me, Alvaro, requires only an act of will.

Indeed, I even regret that submitting to you required coercion. In the course of time, were you to misunderstand my zeal, you would be unwise, ungrateful even."

"I know nothing but that I must go. I shall awaken my valet; he must find me money, and then he must go to the post. I shall go to Venice, to Bentinelli, my mother's banker."

"You need money? Fortunately I foresaw the eventuality; I have money to put at your disposal."

"Keep it. If you were a woman, I would be committing a base act by accepting it."

"What I propose is not a gift, it is a loan. Give me an order on your banker; draw up a list of what you owe here. Leave instructions on your desk for Carlo. Write a letter to your commanding officer claiming that a vital matter obliges you to depart without leave. I shall go the post to get you a carriage and horses; but first, Alvaro, forced as I am to separate from you, I am again plunged into all my earlier fears; repeat after me: *Oh Spirit for me linked to a body, and for me alone, I accept your vassalage and grant you my protection.*"

While prescribing this formula, she had thrown herself at my knees, seizing my hand, pressing it and moistening it with tears.

I was beside myself, not knowing which way to turn; I abandoned my hand, which she kissed, and stammered out the words which seemed so important to her; I had scarcely finished than she got to her feet: "I am yours," she cried with rapture; "now I can become the happiest of all beings."

Instantly she threw a long cloak around herself, pulled a large hat over her eyes, and left my bedchamber.

As though stupefied, I found a statement of my debts. I appended an order for Carlo to pay; I counted out the necessary money; to my commanding officer, and one of my closest friends, I wrote letters which they must have found extraordinary. Already the carriage and the postillion's whip were heard at the door.

Biondetta, still muffled in her cloak, returned and rushed me off. Carlo, awakened by the noise, appeared in his chemise. "Go to my desk," I told him, "there you will find my orders." I climbed into the carriage and drove off.

Biondetta had entered the carriage with me and was seated at the front. Once we were out of town, she took off the all-concealing hat. Her hair was held in a crimson net; only the curly ends were visible, like pearls set in coral. Her face, bare of any other ornament, glowed with its own perfection. One might scarcely conceive how such sweetness, candour and innocence could assort with the the intelligence of her gaze. I caught myself making these observations despite myself; and judging them dangerous for my peace of mind, I closed my eyes and tried to sleep.

My attempt was not in vain: sleep stole over me and offered me the most agreeable dreams, those most appropriate to soothing my soul of the frightening and wayward ideas that had been besetting it. Furthermore, my sleep was long and my mother, later, reflecting on my adventures, claimed that such drowsiness had not been natural. At last, when I awoke, I was on the banks of the canal by which one enters Venice.

It was well on into the night; I felt my sleeve being tugged; it was a porter, who wanted to take my packages. I did not even have a nightcap.

Biondetta appeared at another door, to tell me that the

boat which was to transport me was ready. I got out mechanically, climbed into the felucca and fell once more into my lethargy.

What can I say? The following morning I found myself lodged on St Mark's Square, in the finest apartment in the best inn in Venice. I recognized it immediately. Finding linen and a rich *robe de chambre* next to my bed, I suspected that this could have been a considerate act on the part of the innkeeper at whose establishment I had arrived quite unprovided for.

I got up and peered around to see whether I was the only living object in the room; I was seeking Biondetta.

Ashamed of this first impulse, I gave thanks for my good fortune. So this spirit and I were not joined for ever; I was delivered of it; and after my imprudence, if I were to lose only my position in the guards, I would have to account myself lucky.

Courage, Alvaro, I went on; there are other courts, other sovereigns than those of Naples; let this be a lesson to you, if you are not incurable; henceforth you will be a better man. If your services are rejected, a tender-hearted mother, the Estremadura and a decent inheritance await you.

But what does that imp want of you, inseparable from you for twenty-four hours as he has been? He has taken on a most seductive form; he gave you money, and you must repay him.

Even as I was talking, my creditor appeared; he was bringing me two servants and two gondoliers.

"You must be looked after until Carlo arrives," he said. "The people at the inn vouch for the intelligence and loyalty of these people; you see before you the bravest boatmen of the Republic."

"I approve your choice, Biondetta," I told her; "are you lodging here too?"

"I," replied the page, eyes lowered, "have taken the room furthest from your own in the same apartment, to cause you as little trouble as possible."

This concern for distance between herself and me showed, I felt, consideration and delicacy. I was grateful.

After all, I told myself, I could never deny her the empty air, should she take it into her head to remain invisible in order to haunt me. As long as I know which room she is in, I shall be able to calculate my distance. Pleased with my reasoning, I lightly gave everything my approval.

I now purposed to visit my mother's agent. Biondetta gave her orders for my toilette and, when it was ready, I proceeded about my business.

The agent received me in a manner that occasioned me some surprise. He was in his bank; he cast me an affectionate look from a distance and came towards me.

"Don Alvaro," he said, "I did not know that you were here. Your arrival is most timely, since it prevents me from making a blunder: I was about to send you two letters and some money."

"My quarterly allowance?" I asked.

"Yes," he said "and something else besides. Here are two hundred sequins in addition, which arrived this morning. An old gentleman, to whom I gave a receipt, handed them over to me from dona Mencia. Not having heard from you, she thought you must be ill, and asked a Spaniard of my acquaintance to give them to me to pass on to you."

"Did she tell you his name?"

"It is written on the receipt: don Miguel Pimiento, who

says he was a servant in your household. Since I did not know of your arrival here, I did not ask for his address".

I took the money and opened the letters; my mother was lamenting her poor health, and did not mention the sequins she had sent me; that made me all the more appreciative of her generosity.

Seeing my purse so well and opportunely garnished, I went gaily back to the inn; I had difficulty in locating the modest quarters where Biondetta had taken refuge, and which she would enter by a private passage some way from my door. I came upon it by chance, and saw her bending over near a window, absorbed in reassembling and pasting together the parts of a harpsichord.

"I have money," I told her, "so here is what you lent me." She blushed, as she always did before speaking; she looked for my bond, handed it to me, took the sum and contented herself with saying I was too punctilious, and that she would have liked to extend further the pleasure of having obliged me.

"But I am still in your debt," I told her, "for it was you who paid for the post-horses". She had the relevant account on the table; I paid it and was about to leave the room with apparent sang-froid then she asked me for her orders. I had none to give her, and she went calmly back to her task, turning her back on me. I watched her for some time; she seemed deeply engrossed, working with as much skill as rapidity.

I went back to ponder in my room: "Here," I told myself, "we have the equivalent of that Calderon who lit Soberano's pipe, and although the page looks very distinguished, he springs from the same stock. If he does not render himself either demanding or inconvenient, if he makes no claims, why should I not keep him? Furthermore, he assures me that an act of will is all that is needed to send him away. Why wish now what I can wish at any moment of the day?" My reflections were interrupted by the announcement that dinner was served.

I sat down at table. Biondetta, in full livery, was behind my seat, eager to anticipate my every need. I did not have to turn round to see her: three mirrors arranged throughout the room echoed her every movement. When the dinner was over and the table cleared, she withdrew.

The innkeeper, whom I had met before, came up into my room. It was carnival time, and thus there was nothing surprising in my arrival. He congratulated me on the addition to my retinue, which implied an improvement in my fortunes, and fell back upon praise of my page, the most handsome, affectionate and gentle young man he had ever seen. He asked me if I was intending to take part in the pleasures of carnival: such indeed was my intention. I selected a disguise and climbed into my gondola.

I went to the theatre, and the Ridotto, where I gambled, won forty sequins and returned home rather late, having sought frivolity everywhere I imagined I might find it.

My page, a torch in his hand, welcomed me at the foot of the stairs, handed me over to the attentions of a valet de chambre and retired, after asking me at what time I required his presence in my room. At the usual hour, I answered, without thinking what I was saying and failing to remark that no one was acquainted with my daily habits.

I awoke late the following morning, and promptly arose. By chance my eye fell upon my mother's letter lying on the table. "Estimable woman!" I cried out; "What am I doing here? Why do I not take refuge in your wise counsel? I will, I will, it is my only hope!"

As I was speaking aloud, someone observed that I was awake; someone entered my room, and again I saw the shoal which endangered my reason. He looked serene, modest, submissive and thus to me all the more dangerous. He announced the imminent arrival of a tailor and some cloth; the business expedited, he disappeared with the tailor until luncheon.

I ate little, and hastened to plunge myself into the whirlwind of the city's diversions. I sought out masked figures; I listened, I made cool pleasantries, concluded the evening at the opera and then at gaming, hitherto my chief passion. I won more during this second session than during the first.

Ten days passed in the same mood of heart and mind, and in more or less the same diversions; I met old acquaintances and made new ones. I was introduced to the most distinguished gatherings and admitted to the parties of the nobles in their casinos.

All would have gone well, had my luck at the gaming tables held, but I lost the 1300 sequins I had amassed in one evening at the Ridotto. Rarely can such misfortune have befallen a player. At three in the morning I retired, penniless, owing one hundred sequins to my acquaintances. My chagrin was written on my features, in my whole comportment. Biondetta seemed visibly affected, but she did not say a word.

The next day I arose late and stumped up and down my room. Breakfast was served, but I ate nothing. When it was cleared away, Biondetta remained, contrary to her usual practice. She looked at me for a moment and let fall some tears: "You lost money, don Alvaro; perhaps more than you can repay..."

"And were that to be so, where might I find the remedy?"

"You have no faith: my services are ever yours, and under the same conditions; but they would not be very far-reaching if they extended merely to making you contract such obligations with me as you would feel obliged to fulfill immediately. Be good enough to allow me to take a seat; emotion prevents my remaining standing; furthermore, I have important things to say to you. Do you want to ruin yourself? Why do you gamble so furiously, since you do not know how to play?"

"Does anyone know how to play games of chance? Could someone teach me to do better?"

"Yes; prudence aside, one does learn how to play games of luck, which you improperly call games of chance. There is no chance in this world: everything always has been and always will be a succession of inevitable coincidences which can be understood only through the science of numbers, whose principles are at once so abstract and so deep, that no one can grasp them unless he is guided by a master; but this master must be chosen with skill, and grappled to his pupil. I can communicate this sublime knowledge to you only by an image. The concatenation of numbers creates the rhythm of the universe, rules both what are called fortuitous events and those that are allegedly pre-determined, causing them, through invisible balance-wheels, to occur each in their turn, from all that is truly important in the remote sphere, down to the pitiable little bits of chance which have to-day denuded you of your money."

This scientific tirade in a childlike mouth, this somewhat brusque proposal to give me a master, brought about a slight shiver, a little of that cold sweat which had seized me under the vault at Portici. I looked squarely at Biondetta, who lowered her eyes. "I do not want a master," I told her; "I would be afraid of learning too much; but by all means try to prove to me that a gentleman can use a little superior knowledge at gaming without compromising his character". She took up the challenge:

"The bank functions on the basis of an exorbitant profit which is renewed at every deal; if she did not run risks, the Republic would manifestly be stealing from individuals. But the calculations that the players can make are taken into account, and the bank is always the winner, pitted against one shrewd person among 10,000 dupes."

Conviction was pushed even further. I was taught one single combination, apparently very simple: I could not guess at its principles, but that evening I experienced its infallibility.

In a word, by following Biondetta's instructions I won back all I had lost, made good my gambling debts and, on returning, repaid the money she had lent me to try my luck.

I was in funds, but more embarrassed than ever. I was by now deeply mistrustful as to the intentions of the dangerous being whose services I had accepted. I did not know whether I would be capable of dismissing her; at all events I did not have the strength of mind to do so now. I averted my eyes so as to remain ignorant of her whereabouts, and saw her everywhere where she was not.

Gambling was ceasing to offer an engaging diversion. Faro, which I had loved passionately, no longer being spiced by risk, had lost all its savour for me. The antics of carnival time bored me; I found its sights insipid. Even had I been sufficiently fancy-free to wish to form a liaison with one of the ladies of high degree, I was disheartened in advance by the langour, the ceremonial and the constraints of the role of *cavalier servente*. My only resource was the noblemen's casinos, where I no longer wished to play, and the company of courtesans.

Among this latter kind there were some who were distinguished for the elegance of their adornments and the sprightliness of their manner rather than for their personal charms. In their houses I enjoyed a true freedom, a noisy gaiety which could benumb, if it did not delight, in a word, a continual abuse of reason which freed me for a few moments from the shackles of my own. I paid compliments to all the women of this kind into whose presence I was admitted, without having designs on any; but the most celebrated of them had designs on me, which she soon expressed.

She was known as Olympia, and was twenty-six years of age, very beautiful, talented and witty. She soon let me perceive her penchant for me and, without returning her inclinations, I gave myself to her to find some release from myself.

Our liaison began suddenly and, as it held little allure for me, I imagined that it would end in the same way and that Olympia, bored by my half-heartedness, would soon seek out a lover who would do her greater justice, all the more so since we had embarked on our involvement in the most dispassionate spirit; but our stars decided otherwise. The chastisement of this proud and impulsive woman, and my own further embroilment, doubtless required that she should conceive for me an unbridled passion.

Already I was no longer free to return to my inn of an evening; during the day I was spied upon and overwhelmed with love letters and messages. My coolness was the subject of much complaint. Her jealousy, which had not as yet found an object, was directed towards all the women who might attract my attentions, and would have demanded positively uncivil behaviour towards them on my part, had my nature been more malleable. I did not enjoy this perpetual torment, but I had to live with it. I tried in good faith to love Olympia, purely for the sake of loving, and to distract myself from the dangerous penchant I know myself to be harbouring. Yet an even more explosive episode lay in store.

On Olympia's orders I was secretly observed at my inn. "For how long," she said to me one day, " have you had this page who interests you so much, for whom you show such consideration, and whom you gaze at so fixedly when you order him to your apartment? Why do you oblige him to observe this austere retirement? For he is never seen about Venice."

"My page," I replied, "is a well-born young man, whose education I have taken upon myself out of duty. He is..."

"He," she retorted, her eyes ablaze with anger, "is a woman. You traitor. One of my men saw her through the keyhole, dressing."

"I give you my word of honour that he is no woman..."

"Do not add lying to treachery. This woman has been seen weeping, she is not happy. You do nothing but break the heart of those who give themselves to you. You have abused her, as you abuse me, and you are abandoning her. Send this young person back to her parents, and if your prodigality has prevented you from treating her as she deserves, then she shall receive her due from me. She is entitled to a certain standing in life; I shall see to it that she gets it; but I want her to leave to-morrow."

"Olympia," I resumed, as coldly as I could,"I have sworn to you, and I shall do so again, that this is no woman; and God forbid..."

"What is the meaning of these lies and this "God forbid..." you monster? Send her away, I tell you, or... But I have other resources; I shall unmask you, and she shall listen to reason, if you cannot."

Exhausted by this torrent of tears and threats, but pretending to be unmoved, I retired to my own quarters, although it was late.

My arrival appeared to surprise the servants, and Biondetta in particular; she showed some concern about my health; I replied that it was unimpaired. I had scarcely spoken to her since my liaison with Olympia, and there had been no change in her conduct towards me, but her face betrayed her: her physiognomy was touched with dejection and melancholy.

The next day, hardly had I risen, than Biondetta came into my room, an open letter in her hand. She handed it to me, and I read:

TO THE ONE WHO CALLS HIMSELF BIONDETTO

"I do not know who you are, nor what you may be doing in the company of don Alvaro; but you are too young not to be forgiven, and you are in hands too wicked not to arouse compassion. This gentleman has undoubtedly promised you what he promises everyone, what he swears to me each day, although bent on betraying us. It is said that you are as wise as you are beautiful; you will therefore be open to good advice. You are of an age, Madame, when you can right the wrong you may have done yourself; a sensitive soul now offers you the means to do so. The price of the sacrifice necessary for your well-being is high: it must befit your condition, the notions you have been forced to abandon and those you may have for the future; and you must lay down your terms. If you persist in wishing to be deceived and unhappy, and in causing others to be the same, you must expect the most violent responses that despair can dictate to a rival. I await your reply."

I handed the letter back to Biondetta. "Answer this woman telling her that she is mad," I told her, "and you know better than I do just how true that is."

"You know her, don Alvaro, do you not fear what she may do?"

"I fear only that she may continue worrying me further, and therefore I am leaving her; and to rid myself of her the more surely, I am going this very morning to rent a charming villa I have been offered on the Brenta." I dressed then and there, and went out to conclude my negotiations. On my way, I reflected on Olympia's threats. Poor demented creature! I said, she wants the death of... but for some reason, I could not pronounce that name.

As soon as I had finished my business, I returned to my lodgings; fearing that force of habit might impel me to visit the courtesan, I determined to remain in the apartment for the whole day.

I took up a book, but incapable of applying myself to

reading, I put it down again; I went to the window, and the throng, the motley sights, offended me instead of distracting me. I strode up and down my apartment, seeking peace of mind while experiencing unremitting physical turmoil.

In this irresolute wandering my steps took me to a dark closet, where my servants stored certain necessities not immediately required for my service. I had never been inside it before. I liked the darkness of the place and sat down on a chest, remaining there for some minutes.

After a little time I heard noises in an adjacent room; a line of light shining in my eyes drew me towards a blocked door; it was coming through the keyhole, to which I put my eye.

I saw Biondetta seated at her harpsichord, arms crossed in an attitude of profound reverie. She broke the silence, saying:

"Biondetta! Biondetta! He calls me Biondetta. It is the first, the only tender word he has ever uttered."

She fell silent, and seemed to relapse into her reverie. Then she laid her hands on the harpsichord I had seen her mending. She had a closed book before her on the stand, and now she played an introduction and sang softly, to her own accompaniment.

I instantly understood that she was improvising. Listening more closely, I heard my name, together with that of Olympia: she was improvising in prose upon her supposed situation, upon that of her rival, which she found much happier than her own; and lastly upon my harshness towards her, and my misgivings, which caused a distrust that drew me away from my true happiness. She would have led me down the path to greatness, fortune and learning, and I in my turn would have been all her joy. "Alas," she was saying, "I fear this is no longer possible. My faint charms could not hold him, were he to know me for what I truly am. Whereas a mortal woman..."

Passion was carrying her away, and her voice seemed choked by tears. She rose, took a handkerchief, dried her eyes and went back to the instrument; she was about to sit down again but, the seat having been uncomfortably low, she took the book which was on her stand, put it on the stool and once more played an introduction.

I soon realized that the second musical performance would not resemble the first. I recognized the tune of a barcarolle, presently very fashionable in Venice. She repeated it twice; then, in a clearer and more assured voice, she sang the following verses:

Oh what vain hopes I cherish here,
Daughter of heaven and of the air!
Abandoning the aery sphere
For Alvaro, and for the earth.
My brightness dimmed, in tyranny,
I stoop to abject slavery;
My recompense pray now observe:
I am disdained, and yet I serve.
But lo, the hand that drives you, steed,
Caresses you while urging speed.
You are held captive, it is true,
Yet people fear to injure you.
The rein which holds you in its power
Cannot debase you, cannot lower.
Alvaro, another holds your heart
And keeps our paths so far apart.

THE DEVIL IN LOVE

Tell me, I pray you, by what boldness
She has overcome your coldness?
No one doubts she is sincere,
Oh, she is honest, that is clear.
She pleases where I cannot please.
Suspicion lights on me with ease.
Distrust empoisons now my kindness.
How may I fight against such blindness?
In my presence I am slated,
In my presence I am hated.
Every slight imagined is,
My groans are petty, without cause.
Should I speak out, then woe is me;
My silence, though, is treachery.
Love, you set up this counterfeit;
I play the mistress of deceit.
So to avenge our so sore wrong
Dispel his errors ere too long.
Unveil me to the ungrateful one
And whatsoe'er it pick upon,
All tenderness abhorred be
That is not tenderness for me.
My rival's all-triumphant state
Makes her the mistress of my fate.
And I perforce can only wait
For exile, or for death's grim date.
In vain tear not yourself apart,
You motions of a jealous heart.
Hatred is all you could awake.
And so, keep silent, for love's sake.

The sound of her voice, the melody, the implication of

the lines and the turn of phrase all threw me into ineffable confusion. "Extravagant being, dangerous imposter," I cried, hastily retreating from that place where I had stayed too long. Could anyone don the traits of truth and nature more skilfully? How fortunate I was to have discovered this keyhole only to-day! How eagerly would I have come here to intoxicate myself, how I would have contributed to my own self-deception! I had to leave, to go to the Brenta to-morrow at the latest, indeed this very evening!

I immediately called a servant, and had a gondola loaded with such things as I needed to spend the night in my new abode.

It would have been impossible for me to await nightfall in my inn. I went out and walked at random. At a street turning, I thought I saw Bernardillo going into a café, Bernardillo who had been with Soberano on our walk to Portici. "Another phantom!" said I; "they are pursuing me." I climbed into my gondola and rode through all of Venice, from canal to canal; it was eleven o'clock when I returned. I wanted to leave for the Brenta, and as my weary gondoliers refused their services, I was obliged to call for others; they arrived, and my servants, informed of my intentions, went before me into the gondola, bearing their own belongings. Biondetta was following me.

Hardly had I stepped into the boat than cries forced me to turn round. A masked figure was stabbing Biondetta: "You have defeated me! So you must die then, hateful rival!"

The action was so sudden that even one of the gondoliers who had remained ashore was powerless to stop it. He tried to attack the assassin by raising a torch to his eyes; another masked figure ran up and drove him back with a threatening motion, and a thunderous voice which I thought I recognized as that of Bernardillo was heard. Beside myself, I leapt from the gondola, but the murderers had disappeared. By the light of the torch I discovered Biondetta, pale, steeped in her own blood; dying.

My state was indescribable. All other thoughts drained away.

What I saw now was a woman adored, the victim of an absurd prejudice, sacrificed to my vain and extravagant temperament and crushed, hitherto, by the most cruel insults.

I rushed forward, calling for assistance and vengeance at one and the same time. Attracted by the noise of these events, a surgeon appeared. I had the wounded creature transported to my apartment and, for fear that sufficient care might not be taken, I myself shared the burden.

When they had undressed her, and I saw that lovely bleeding body with its two gaping wounds, both seeming to threaten the sources of life itself, I said and committed a thousand extravagances.

Biondetta, presumed to be unconscious, could not have heard them; but the innkeeper and his men, a surgeon and two doctors summoned for the occasion, judged that it would be dangerous to allow me to be left at her side, and dragged me from the room. My servants were left beside me, but one of them having unwisely informed me that the doctors had pronounced the wound to be fatal, I began to emit shrill cries.

Exhausted at last by my transports, I fell into a dejection which gave way to sleep.

It seemed to me that I saw my mother in a dream: I was telling her of my adventure and, to render it more vivid, I was leading her towards the ruins of Portici.

"Let us not go there, my son," she said to me, "you are clearly in danger." As we were passing through a narrow defile, which I was walking through quite boldly, a hand suddenly thrust me towards a precipice, a hand I recognized as that of Biondetta. I was falling, but another hand pulled me back, and I found myself in my mother's arms. I awoke, still panting with terror. "Devoted, fond, tender, loving mother," I cried, "you do not desert me, even in my dreams".

Biondetta! Do you wish to ruin me? But my dream was wrought by my own troubled imagination. Ah, let us drive away such ideas as would cause me to be lacking in gratitude and humanity.

I called a servant and asked for news: the two surgeons were keeping vigil, having drawn much blood and fearing the onset of fever.

The next day, after the implements had been removed, it was decided that the wounds were dangerous only in that they were so deep; but fever struck, soared, and the patient had to be exhausted by more bleeding.

I was so insistent that I should be let into the apartment, that they could not but grant me my wish.

Biondetta was delirious, and was ceaselessly repeating my name; never had she seemed more beautiful.

Do I indeed see here what I took to be a many-coloured phantom, I wondered, a mass of shining vapours assembled purely to impress my senses?

Surely she was mortal, just as I was, and was dying because I had always refused to heed her, because I wilfully exposed her to danger. I was a brute, a monster.

If you die, most worthy object of my love (thought I), creature whose goodness I have so signally failed to recognize, I do not want to survive you. I too shall die, after having sacrificed the barbarous Olympia on your tomb.

If you are given back to me, I shall be yours; I shall recognize the blessings you impart; I shall crown your virtues and your patience, and shall bind myself to you with indissoluble links, vowing to make your happiness through the blind sacrifice of my feelings and my desires.

I shall not describe the painful efforts made by science and nature to recall to life a body which seemed bound to succumb in the face of the expedients deployed for its relief.

Three weeks passed in a battle pitched between fear and hope; at last the fever fell away, and it seemed that the invalid was regaining consciousness.

I called her my dear Biondetta and she gripped my hand; from that moment, she recognized everything around her. I was at her bedside and she turned her eyes upon me, mine being wet with tears. I would be quite unequal to describing the grace and expression of her smile as she looked at me: "Dear Biondetta," she repeated; "I am don Alvaro's dear Biondetta."

She wanted to say more, but once again I was told to withdraw. I decided to remain in her room, but concealed from her view. At last I received permission to approach. "Biondetta," I told her, "I am having your assassins pursued."

"Ah, spare them," she said. "they are the source of all my happiness. Now I am yours, both in life and death."

I have my reasons for cutting short descriptions of these tender scenes which passed between us until such time as the doctors assured me that I could have Biondetta moved to the banks of the Brenta, where the air would be better suited to restoring her strength. As soon as her sex had been ascertained by the need to dress her wounds, I had employed two women to attend to her. I gathered around her everything that might contribute to her comfort, and devoted myself solely to her relief, amusement and pleasure.

Her strength was visibly returning, and each day her beauty seemed to take on new lustre. At last, thinking I could engage her in a conversation of some importance without detriment to her health, I said to her: "Biondetta, I am overwhelmed with love; I am persuaded that you are not an imaginary being, and I am convinced that you love me, despite my outrageous conduct towards you until this moment. But you know that my worries were not without foundation. Explain to me the mysteries of the strange apparition which distressed my gaze in the vault at Portici. Whence came that frightful monster, and the little bitch which preceded your arrival, and what became of them? How and why did you replace them and become attached to me? Who were they, and who are you? Pray reassure a heart that is all yours."

"Alvaro," replied Biondetta, "astonished by your boldness, the necromancers decided to seek amusement from your humiliation and to use terror to reduce you to the state of an abject slave of their desires. As a foretaste of fear, they provoked you to conjure up the most powerful and redoubtable of all their spirits; and, with the help of those whose rank is subject to their own, they presented you with a sight which would have caused you to expire with terror, had the vigour of your spirit not caused their stratagem to turn against them.

At your heroic countenance Sylphs, Salamanders, Gnomes and Undines, enchanted by your courage, resolved to give you the advantage over your enemies.

I am a Sylph by origin, and one of the most extraordinary among their number. I appeared to you in the guise of the little bitch; I received your orders, and we all hastened to fulfill them. The more hauteur, resoluteness, nonchalance and intelligence you put into the regulation of your movements, the more our zeal and admiration for you increased.

You ordered me to serve you as your page, to amuse you as a singer. I submitted joyfully, and tasted such sweet fruit in my obedience that I resolved to obey you for ever.

Let us, I told myself, make a decision as to my state and happiness. Abandoned in the empty airs to inevitable uncertainty, denied sensation and enjoyment, a slave to the cabbalists' spells, a creature of their whim, limited in my faculties as in my perceptions, should I waver further as to the choice of the means through which I could ennoble my essence?

I am permitted to take on a body in order to associate myself with a wise man. Behold that man. If I lower myself to the condition of a mere woman, if through this voluntary change I lose the natural rights of the Sylph and the company of my companions, in exchange I shall enjoy the happiness of loving and of being loved. I shall serve my conqueror, I shall instruct him on the sublimeness of his being, of whose privileges he is ignorant. With the powers whose dominion I shall have relinquished, he will subdue all the spirits of the spheres. He is made to be king of the world, and I shall be its queen.

These thoughts, more surprising than you might imagine in a being devoid of bodily substance, instantly convinced me.

I would take on a woman's body and abandon it only with life itself.

When I had taken on a body, Alvaro, I perceived that I had a heart. I admired you, I loved you; but what was my state, when I saw in you only repugnance and hatred? I could neither change, nor even turn back; a victim of all the reverses your kind are subject to, having brought upon myself the anger of the spirits and the implacable hatred of the necromancers, without your protection I would have become the unhappiest being under the sun. What am I saying? I would be so still without your love."

The thousand graces of her face, her movements, the sound of her voice, added to the wonder of this compelling speech. I could understand nothing of what I was hearing. But what was comprehensible in this whole adventure?

All this seemed like a dream, I told myself; but is human life anything else? I dreamed more curiously than the next man, that was all.

I had seen her with my own eyes, awaiting all the succour that science could bring, almost at the gates of death, passing through all the stages of exhaustion and pain.

Man was an assemblage of a little mud and water. Why should woman not be made of dew, terrestrial vapours and moonbeams, the concentrated remains of a rainbow?

What is possible, what impossible?

The result of my reflections was that I surrendered even more completely to my inclinations, while believing I was following my reason. I showered Biondetta with attentions, innocent caresses. She accepted them with an openness that enchanted me, with that natural modesty that needs no prior reflection or alarm.

A month sped by, spent in intoxicating tenderness. Biondetta, entirely recovered, was able to accompany me everywhere on my outings. I had a riding habit made for her and wearing this garment, and a big plumed hat, she made all heads turn. Wherever we went, my beloved was inevitably the envy of all those fortunate citizens who people the enchanted banks of the Brenta in fine weather; even the women seemed to have forsworn the jealousy of which they are accused, whether conquered by a superiority they could not deny, or disarmed by a bearing which bespoke complete unawareness of its advantages.

Known to all as the lover of so ravishing an object, my pleasure equalled my love, and I felt even more elated when I chanced to pride myself on the nature of its origin.

I could not doubt but that she possessed the rarest knowledge, and I had reason to suppose that her aim was to bestow it upon me; but she talked to me only of everyday things, and seemed to have lost this other aim from view. "Biondetta," I said one evening as we were walking on the terrace of my garden, "when some strangely flattering inclination persuaded you to link your fate with mine, you promised to make me worthy of you by imparting to me knowledge which is not vouchsafed to the common run of men. Do I seem to you unworthy of your attentions? Can a love as tender, as delicate as yours, have no desire to ennoble its object?"

"Oh, Alvaro," she replied, "I have been a woman for six months, and I feel that my passion has not lasted a day. Forgive me if the sweetest of sensations has intoxicated a heart which has never throbbed before. I would like to show you how to love as I love; and this sentiment alone would raise you above your kind. But human pride aspires to other enjoyments; its natural disquiet prevents it from laying hold of any happiness if it cannot envisage a greater one in the offing. Yes, Alvaro, I shall instruct you. I was forgetting my own interests, and happily; yet I must instruct you, for I must rediscover my greatness in your own; but it is not enough for you to promise to be mine: you must give yourself unreservedly and for ever."

We were seated upon a stretch of greensward, under a bower of honeysuckle at the end of the garden; I threw myself at her knees. "Dear Biondetta," I said, "I swear unfailing devotion."

"No," she said, "you do not know me; you must abandon yourself to me completely. That alone will reassure me and suffice."

I kissed her hand in an ecstasy of joy, and redoubled my vows; she countered them with her fears. In the heat of the conversation our heads bowed and our lips met... At that moment I felt myself seized by the coat-tails, and shaken by a strange force...

It was my dog, a young great Dane I had been given, whom I amused daily by letting him play with my handkerchief. As he had escaped from the house the previous evening, I had had him tied up to prevent further mishap. He had just broken free of his chain, had found me, guided by his sense of smell, and was pulling me by the coat to demonstrate his joy and to encourage me to further frolics. In vain I sought to fend him off with my hands, with my commands: he ran around me and came back to me, barking. Finally defeated by his importunity, I seized him by the collar and led him back to the house.

As I was returning to the bower to rejoin Biondetta, a servant walking almost on my heels informed me that dinner was served, so we went to take our places at table. A tête-à-tête might have been embarrassing for Biondetta, but fortunately a third person was present, a young nobleman who had come to spend the evening with us.

The next day I went to Biondetta's apartment determined to inform her of the serious reflections which had occupied me during the night. She was still in bed, and I sat down beside her.

"Yesterday," I said, "we almost engaged in an act which I might have regretted to the end of my days. My mother is insisting that I should marry. I could not be anyone but yours, and can make no serious commitment without her consent. Regarding you already as my wife, dear Biondetta, my duty is to respect you."

"Indeed! Must I not in turn respect you, Alvaro? But might not this sentiment be the canker of love?"

"You are wrong," I replied, "it is love's zest..."

"A fine zest, which brings you to me with so cool an air, and quite chills me! Ah, Alvaro, Alvaro! Fortunately I am free as air, I have neither father nor mother, and I would love with all my heart without that particular zest. It is only natural that you should respect your mother; it is right that she should give her blessing to the union of our hearts, but why should blessing precede union? With you, prejudices are born for want of enlightenment and, whether through a process of reasoning or not, they render your conduct as inconsistent as it is bizarre. While subjected to real duties, you impose others upon yourself which are unnecessary or impossible to fulfill; in a word, you seek to stray from the true path in the pursuit of the object whose possession you most desire. Our union becomes dependent on the will of others. Who knows if dona Mencia will find me of sufficiently high lineage to ally myself with the house of Maravillas? And would I not feel belittled were I to have to secure you from her instead of possessing you of your own accord? Is it a man destined for great knowledge who is speaking to me, or a child just out of the mountains of the Estremadura? And must my sensitivities go unheeded because others' are being considered more than my own? Alvaro, Alvaro! The Spanish notion of love is for ever being vaunted; yet the Spaniard will always demonstrate pride and arrogance rather than love!"

I had seen extraordinary scenes in my time but I was quite unprepared for this one. I wanted to explain my respect for my mother which was prescribed by duty but inspired even more by gratitude and attachment. My protestations went unheeded. "I did not become a woman for nothing, Alvaro: I gave myself to you freely and I wish you to give yourself in the same way. Let dona Mencia dissaprove afterwards, if she is deprived of reason. Talk of this no more. I am respected, we respect one another, everyone is respected - with all this respect, I am becoming unhappier that when I was shunned." And she began to sob.

Luckily mine was a proud character, and this trait

protected me from the impulse of weakness which was drawing me to Biondetta's feet in an attempt to disarm this unreasonable anger, and to stem those tears the mere sight of which threw me into a state of despair. I retired to my study, and had someone chained me to a chair at that moment, they would have been doing me a service. At last, fearing the outcome of the struggle, I ran to my gondola, encountering one of Biondetta's serving women on the way. "I am going to Venice, " I told her, "I am needed there for the furthering of the lawsuit brought about by Olympia;" and I left then and there, a prey to galloping unease, ill-pleased with Biondetta and even more so with myself, seeing that my only remaining options were cowardly or desperate.

When I reached the city, I landed at the first *calle*; I rushed bewildered through all the alleys on my way, not even noticing that a frightful storm was brewing and that I should start to think about finding shelter. It was mid-day, and soon I was caught in a downfall of heavy rain mingled with copious hail. I saw an open door before me, that of the church of the great Franciscan convent, and took refuge within.

My first reflection was that it had taken an incident of this kind to drive me into a church for the first time since my stay in Venice; the second was to make good this total forgetfulness of my duties.

At last, wishing to drag myself from my thoughts, I considered the paintings and attempted to look at the monuments, embarking on a sort of voyage of discovery around the nave and choir.

Finally I came to an obscure chapel lit by a lamp, since daylight could not reach it: a monument at the end of this chapel struck me deeply.

Two genies were laying a female form into a tomb of white marble, while two others were weeping nearby. All the figures were of white marble, and their natural brightness, heightened by the contrast with the surrounding gloom, reflecting the faint light of the lamp, seemed to make them shine with a light of their own, which itself illuminated the chapel's end.

I approached and contemplated the figures; they seemed to me wonderfully proportioned, full of expression and executed in a most accomplished manner.

I gazed upon the head of the main figure, and what did I see? It was as though I were looking at a portrait of my mother. I was seized by a sharp yet tender pain, a holy sense of respect.

"Oh mother! Does this cold simulacrum here take on your beloved appearance in order to warn me that my lack of affection and the disorder of my life will lead you to the grave? Oh most estimable of women? Though he may be adrift, your Alvaro still acknowledges that you hold sway over his heart. He would rather die a thousand deaths than stray from the obedience he owes you. Alas, I am devoured by the most tyrannical of passions: which it is now impossible for me to master. You have just spoken to my heart and, if I must banish it, teach me how I may do so without it costing me my life."

While forcefully uttering this urgent invocation, I had prostrated myself with my face to the ground, and in this attitude I awaited the reply which I was almost certain I would receive, so transported was I.

I reflect now, though I was in no state to do so then, that on all occasions when we need especial help in regulating our conduct, if we ask for it strongly enough (even though our wishes may not be granted), at least, in the desire to receive it, we enable ourselves to draw upon the resources of our prudence. Here is what mine duly proposed to me:

"You must put a sense of duty, and considerable physical space, between your passion and yourself; events will enlighten you."

"Let us depart," I said, rising hastily, "I shall open my heart to my mother, I shall put myself once more in her beloved care."

I returned to my usual inn, looked for a carriage and, without encumbering myself with a retinue, I took the road to Turin to enter Spain via France; but first I put a three hundred zecchino note, drawn on my bank, in a packet, along with the following letter:

TO MY DEAR BIONDETTA

"I am tearing myself away from you, my dear Biondetta, and it would be like tearing myself from life itself, were my heart not comforted by the hope of the speediest return. I am going to see my mother: inspired by your charming idea, I shall win her over, and return with her consent to our forming a union which is certain to make my happiness. Pleased to have fulfilled my duty before giving myself over entirely to love, I shall devote the rest of my life to you. You will be making the acquaintance of a Spaniard, my Biondetta; you may judge from his conduct that, if he obeys the duties of honour and of family ties, he can also satisfy the other duties. Observing the happy outcome of his old-fashioned ideas, you will not judge his attachment to them as mere pride. I cannot doubt your love, which swore total obedience to me, but I shall recognize this love even further through your gentle acquiescence to views whose sole object is our common happiness. I am sending you only what may be needed for the upkeep of our house. From Spain I shall send you what I think to be worthy of you, in the expectation that the keennest tenderness ever will bring you back your slave for eternity."

I was on the road to Estremadura: the year was at its loveliest and everything seemed to lend itself to my impatience to reach my native country. I could already make out the bell towers of Turin when, a somewhat dishevelled poste-chaise having passed my vehicle, it stopped and afforded me a glimpse, through a window, of a woman gesticulating and on the point of climbing out.

My postillion stopped of his own accord; I got out, and found Biondetta in my arms, where she remained in a swoon, having been able to utter but these few words: "Alvaro! You abandoned me!"

I carried her to my chaise, the only place where I could seat her comfortably, since fortunately it had two seats. I did all I could to help her to breath more easily, freeing her of those garments that were incommoding her and, supporting her in my arms, I continued my journey in a state that may be imagined.

We stopped at the first respectable inn, and I had Biondetta carried into the most comfortable room, where I had her laid upon a bed, and sat down beside her. I had ordered spirits and elixirs of the kind suited to dispelling a fainting fit, and at last she opened her eyes.

"Once again, someone is seeking my death," she said; "someone will soon be satisfied."

"What injustice," I retorted. "Some whim causes you to refuse to accede to certain steps that I sincerely feel necessary on my part. I would be in danger of failing in my duty if I could not hold out against you, and I am exposing myself to unpleasantness and remorse which might trouble the tranquillity of our union. I chose to escape in order to seek my mother's consent..."

"And why did you not inform me of your intention, cruel one? Have I not vowed to obey you? But to abandon me alone, without protection, to the vengeance of the enemies I have made myself on your behalf, to expose me, as a result of your action, to the most humiliating affronts...."

"Explain yourself, Biondetta. Might someone have dared..."

"And what might anyone be risking with a being of my sex, deprived of any authority as I am, and lacking all assistance? The base Bernardillo had followed us to Venice; hardly had you disappeared than, having ceased to fear you, powerless against me since I became yours but still able to stir the imagination of those in my service, he had your house on the Brenta besieged by phantoms of his own making. My women servants abandoned me in alarm. According to a general rumour, backed up by a number of letters, a sprite had carried off a captain of the King's guard in Naples and brought him to Venice. People maintained that I was this sprite, and indeed it seemed more or less established by this evidence. Everyone shrank from me in horror. I begged for assistance, for compassion, but found none. At last gold succeeded in obtaining what human decency was denied, I was sold a very poor chaise for a high price; I found guides and postillions, and followed you..."

My resolve seemed about to weaken at the tale of Biondetta's misfortunes. "I could not foresee events of this kind," I said. "I had seen you as the object of the consideration and respect of all the inhabitants of the banks of the Brenta; could I have imagined that what seemed so rightfully earned would be withdrawn from you in my absence? Oh Biondetta! you are so clear-sighted; should you not have foreseen that by thwarting views as reasonable as mine, you would drive me to desperate solutions. Why..."

"Is one always in a position to control one's impulses? I am a woman by choice, Alvaro, but I am a woman, open to all impressions; I am not made of marble. I chose the elemental matter of which my earthly body is made; it is susceptible; were it not, I would lack sensitivity; you would cause me to feel nothing and I would cease to be of interest to you. Forgive me for having run the risk of taking on all the imperfections of my sex to unite, if I could, all its graces; but the rash step has been taken, and constituted as I am at present, my responses are incomparably keen: my imagination is volcanic. In a word, I have passions of a violence which should alarm you, were you not the object of the most unshackled of all, and if we did not know the principles and effects of these natural impulses better than they are known in Salamanca. There they are given odious names; there is talk of stifling them, at the very least. To stifle a celestial flame, the only means by which body and soul can act mutually upon one another and force each other to concur in the necessary maintaining of their union - that is foolish, my dear Alvaro! One must regulate these impulses, but sometimes one should yield to them; if they are thwarted they rise up all at once, and reason no longer knows where to stand in order to rule. Spare me in these moments, Alvaro: I am only six months old, I am at the mercy of everything I feel. Remember that a single refusal, a single word spoken without due consideration, stirs up pride, dawning resentment, mistrust, fear; what am I saying? How clearly can I see it - myself a poor lost creature, and my Alvaro as unhappy as I!"

"Oh Biondetta," I began once more, "you are a continual source of astonishment; but I can sense nature herself in your avowal of your inclinations. We shall find the means to combat them in our mutual tenderness. Furthermore, we may put all our trust in the advice of that estimable mother who will receive you in her arms. She will cherish you, I am convinced, and everything will conspire towards our spending happy days together..."

"I must abide by your wishes, Alvaro. I know my sex and do not hope for as much as you do; but, to please you, I shall obey you and put myself in your hands."

Pleased at finding myself on the road to Spain, at Biondetta's response and at being in the company of the object which had captivated my reason and my senses, I was in a hurry to cross the Alps and reach France; but it seemed that the heavens had turned against me since she had joined me: fearful storms delayed my progress, making roads impassable and passes impracticable. The horses stumbled; my carriage, which seemed new and well-assembled, fell apart at every stop and had a faulty axle, or back train, or wheels. At last, after an infinity of set-backs, I reached the col de Tende.

Amidst all these possibilities for disquiet and the obstacles that such a tempestuous journey offered me, I could not but admire the figure cut by Biondetta. She was no longer the tender, sad or passionate woman I had previously known; it was as though she wanted to soothe my anxiety by giving herself over to moments of the greatest gaiety, and to convince me that the stresses and strains held nothing irksome for her.

All this agreeable badinage was mingled with caresses so seductive as to be irresistible. I yielded, but with reservations; my endangered pride acted as a brake to the violence of my desires. She could read my expression too well not to judge of my confusion and so try to increase it. I was in danger, I confess. On one occasion in particular, had a wheel not broken, I do not know what would have become of my honour. That put me a little on my guard for the future.

After incredible exertions, we arrived at Lyon. Out of consideration to Biondetta I agreed to rest there for several days. She drew my attention to the freedom and ease of manner of the French nation. "It is in Paris, at court, that I should like to see you established. Resources of all kinds will be at your disposal; you will be able to cut whatever figure you choose, and I have unfailing means of ensuring that you would triumph; the French are ladies' men and, if I do not presume too much of my appearance, the most distinguished among them would come to pay me homage, while I would sacrifice them all to my Alvaro. A fine victory for that famous Spanish vanity!"

I took this proposition as banter. "No," said she, "I am seriously entertaining the idea."

"Then let us leave quickly for Estremadura," I replied, "to return to present the wife of don Alvaro Maravillas at the court of France, for it would never do to show yourself there as a mere adventuress..."

"I am on the road to Estremadura," she said, "and I

must perforce regard it as the goal where I must find my happiness. What else is there for me?"

I heard and saw her reluctance, but I was proceeding towards my own ends, and soon found myself on Spanish soil. There I was given even less respite from unexpected obstacles - quagmires, impassable ruts, drunken muleteers, restive mules - than I had had in Piedmont and Savoy.

Much ill is spoken of the inns of Spain, and this with good reason; yet I esteemed myself happy when the contretemps experienced during the day did not force me to spend part of the night in the open countryside, or in some sequestered grange.

"What sort of a country are we to find," she said, " to judge by what we are going through? Have we still a long way to go?"

"You are in Estremadura," I told her, "and ten leagues from the castle of Maravillas."

"We shall certainly never reach it; the sky is barring our way. Look at that mist."

I looked at the sky, and never had it seemed more menacing. I observed to Biondetta that our grange could shelter us from the storm. "And from the thunder?" she said.

"What do you fear from thunder, you who are so accustomed to dwelling in the air, who have so often observed its formation and must know its physical origins so well?"

"I would not fear it if I were less familiar with it; I have subjected myself to physical phenomena out of love for you, and I fear them because they kill and because they are physical."

84

We were seated on two heaps of straw at the two ends of the grange. Meanwhile the storm, after having made its presence felt from a distance, was approaching and lowing fearsomely. The sky looked like a fire-pan whipped by the winds in a thousand directions; the thunderclaps, echoing in the caverns of the nearby mountains, reverberated horribly around us. They did not follow one another, they seemed to clash. Wind, rain and hail fought as to which might add most to the horror of the frightful tableau which distressed our senses. A lightning flash seemed to set our shelter ablaze, followed by a terrible thunder clap. Biondetta, her eyes closed, fingers in her ears, rushed into my arms: "Ah, Alvaro, I am lost..."

I tried to reassure her. "Put your hand on my heart," she said. She placed it on her bosom, and although she was ill-advised in causing me to press upon a place where the beating should not have been at its most detectable, I could feel that its movement was indeed extraordinary. She was clutching me with all her strength at every lightning flash. At last a flash occurred even more terrifying than those preceding it: Biondetta took refuge from it in such a way as to ensure that, in the case of mishap, it could not strike her without first striking me.

The effect of this fright seemed strange to me, and I began to fear, not the consequences of the storm, but the outcome of a plot devised in her mind to overcome my resistance to her views. Although more overwhelmed than words can express, I got up: "Biondetta," I told her, "you do not know what you are doing. Calm this fear; this uproar threatens neither you nor me."

My phlegm must have surprised her, but she managed to hide her thoughts from me while continuing to simulate disquiet. Luckily the storm had done its utmost, the sky was clearing, and soon the moon's brightness told us that we no longer had anything to fear from the disorder of the elements.

Biondetta remained on the spot where she had positioned herself. I sat down next to her without profferring a word. She pretended to sleep, and I set to pondering, more sadly than I had done since the beginning of my adventure, on the necessarily problematical outcome of my passion. The bare bones of my reflections were these: my mistress was charming, but I wanted to make her my wife.

Daylight having surprised me in these thoughts, I arose to go and see whether I could continue my journey. But this was impossible, for the moment. The muleteer who was driving my caleche told me that his mules could not be moved at present. While I was in this quandary, Biondetta came up to join me.

I was beginning to lose patience when a man of sinister mien, but vigorously built, appeared before the door of the farm, driving two robust-looking mules before him. I suggested that he drive me to my home; he knew the road, and we agreed upon a price.

I was about to climb back into my carriage, when I thought I recognized a countrywoman who was crossing the road, followed by a manservant. I approached, looking at her fixedly. It was Berthe, a good farmer's wife from my village and the sister of my nurse. I called to her and she stopped, looking at me in her turn, but with an expression of consternation. "What, is it you?" she said to me, "senor don Alvaro! What brings you to a place where your undoing is certain, and to which you have brought desolation?"

"Me! My dear Berthe, what have I done?"

"Ah, senor Alvaro, does not your conscience reproach you for the wretched situation to which your estimable mother, our good mistress, finds herself reduced? She is dying..."

"Dying!" I cried...

"Yes," she continued, "and this as a result of the chagrin you have caused her; even as I speak to you, she is probably dead. Letters have reached her from Naples, from Venice, containing news to make one tremble. Our good lord, your brother, is furious; he says that he will denounce you, deliver you over himself..."

"Well now, Mme Berthe, if you return to Maravillas before me, tell my brother he will be seeing me soon."

Whereupon, the caleche being harnessed, I presented my hand to Biondetta, concealing the turmoil in my soul beneath an appearance of firmness. She, showing herself alarmed, cried out: "What! Are we going to turn ourselves over to your brother? Are we going to embitter an angry family and woe-begone vassals with our presence?"

"I would hardly be afraid of my brother, Madame, if he were imputing to me wrongs I have not done; it is important that I should disabuse him. If I have done wrong, I must excuse myself, and since these wrongs do not come from my heart, I have a right to his compassion and indulgence. If I have led my mother to the grave, I must make amends for this scandal , and bemoan this loss so loudly that the truth, the public nature of my regrets, may wash away the stain with which my unnatural behaviour would taint my blood in the sight of all Spain."

"Ah, don Alvaro, you are rushing headlong to your ruin and my own; these sundry letters, these presumptions broadcast so rashly, so unfairly, are the consequence of our adventures and of the persecution I experienced in Venice. The traitor Bernardillo, insufficiently known to you, is hounding your brother; he will bring him to his ruin..."

"What have I to fear from Bernardillo or from any other coward on this earth? I myself, Madame, am the only enemy I need fear. My brother will never be led to blind vengeance, or to actions unworthy of a man of courage and intelligence, in short, of a gentleman."

This somewhat lively conversation was followed by silence; it could have discountenanced both of us; but after a few moments, Biondetta gradually became drowsy, and fell asleep.

Could I fail to gaze upon her? Could I consider her without emotion? Upon that face, aglow with all perfection, all luxuriance, in a word, with youth, sleep overlaid the natural grace of repose with that delicious living freshness which lends harmony to all features; a new enchantment seized me; it dispelled my distrust; my misgivings were stilled, or rather, my remaining foremost concern was that the head of the object of whom I was enamoured, jolted by the bumpings of the carriage, might not be inconvenienced by their suddenness and roughness. I had to do all I could to support it, to shield it. But then we felt a jolt so violent that it became impossible for me to soften it; Biondetta gave a cry and we were overturned. The axle was broken; the mules, fortunately, had stopped. I disengaged myself: filled with the most intense alarm, I hastened to Biondetta. She had only a slight contusion of the elbow, and soon we were standing in the open countryside, but exposed to the ardour of the mid-day sun, five leagues from my mother's castle, without any apparent means of reaching it, for there was no sign of any habitation whatsoever.

Yet my careful gaze seemed to descry some smoke rising behind a coppice about a league away, mingling among some fairly tall trees; so, entrusting my vehicle to the care of the muleteer, I engaged Biondetta to walk with me in the direction that seemed to offer some semblance of assistance.

The further we advanced, the steadier became our hope; ahead, the little forest seemed to cleave into two; soon it formed an avenue at the end of which the buildings of a modest structure could be perceived; finally, a considerable farm bounded our view.

All seemed to be movement in this dwelling, isolated though it was. As we came into view, a man stepped forward and came towards us.

He approached us civilly. His outward appearance was decent; he was dressed in a black satin doublet slashed with orange, decorated with silver braid. He looked about twenty five to thirty years of age, and had a countryman's complexion. There was a certain freshness beneath the tan, bespeaking vigour and health.

I informed him of the accident which had brought us thither.

"Senor caballero," he replied, "you are most welcome, and among people who are filled with good will. I have a forge here, and your axle can be repaired; but to-day you could give me all the gold of my master the duke of Medina-Sidonia, and neither I nor any of my men would set to work. My wife and I are just back from church: this is our brightest hour. When you see the bride, my relatives, my friends and the neighbours whom I must entertain, you will judge if I could set anyone to work just now. However, if Madame and yourself do not scorn a company which has earned its living honestly since the beginning of the monarchy, we shall sit down at table. We are all happy to-day, and we hope you will share our pleasure. To-morrow we shall think about business".

Then he gave orders for my carriage to be fetched.

So there I was, the guest of Marcos, the duke's tenant-farmer, and we entered the room prepared for the wedding breakfast; adjoining the main house, it occupied the entire far end of the courtyard, a sort of arcaded arbour, decorated with festoons of flowers, whence one's gaze, caught at first by two small copses, lost itself agreeably in the countryside, across the interval formed by the avenue.

The meal was ready. Luisia, the newly-wed, was seated between Marcos and myself; Biondetta was on the other side of Marcos. The parents-in-law and other relatives were opposite, and the young folk at the two ends.

The bride lowered two dark eyes which were not meant for furtive glances; every remark that was made to her, even the most indifferent, caused her to smile and blush.

At the beginning of the meal, gravity presided, for such is the character of the nation; but as the wineskins became less swollen, faces became less solemn. People began to unbend when, suddenly, local improvisers appeared around the table. These were blind men who sang the following couplets, accompanying themselves on their guitars:

THE DEVIL IN LOVE

Marcos said to Luisia:
Will you take my trust and my heart?
She answered, Follow me,
We shall talk in church.
There, with mouth and eyes
They swore to one another
A pure and living flame:
If you are curious
To see a happy couple,
Come to Estremadura.
Luisia is good, she is fair:
Marcos has many rivals;
But he disarms them all,
Proving himself worthy of her;
And here all, with one accord,
Applauding their choice,
Praise a passion so pure.
If you are curious
To see a happy couple,
Come to Estremadura.
Their hearts are united
With a tender sympathy!
Their flocks are together
In the same fold;
Their pains and their pleasures,
Their cares, vows, desires,
Follow the same measures.
If you are curious
To see a happy couple,
Come to Estremadura.

While the company was listening to these songs, which were as simple as those for whom they seemed to be fashioned, all the men servants of the farm, no longer required for service, foregathered gaily to eat the leavings; mingling with the 'Egyptians' summoned to add to the pleasure of the merrymaking, beneath the trees of the avenue they formed groups which embellished our view, and which were as lively as they were motley.

Biondetta was continually seeking out my gaze, forcing me to look in the direction of the objects with which she appeared agreeably preoccupied, seeming to reproach me for quite failing to share with her all the amusement they procured her.

But the meal already seemed to have lasted too long for the young folk, who were waiting for the dancing. Those of a more mature age had to show indulgence. The table was dismantled, the boards which formed it and the casks on which it stood were pushed to the back of the arbour; becoming trestles, they acted as a theatre for the musicians. The Sevillian fandango was played, young gypsy girls danced it with their castanets and tambourines; the wedding guests mingled amongst them, imitating them; the dance had become general.

Biondetta seemed to devour the spectacle with her eyes. Without leaving her seat, she tried out all the movements she saw being performed.

"I do believe," said she, "that I should love dancing to the point of madness." Soon she had joined them and forced me to dance. At first she showed signs of hesitation, even a little clumsiness; but soon she seemed to find her feet and to combine grace and strength with lightness and precision. She was beginning to feel warm;

she needed her handkerchief, my own, any that might come her way; she paused only to mop her brow.

I had never been passionate about dancing; and my soul was not sufficiently free for me to give myself over to so vain an amusement. I withdrew and reached one of the ends of the arbour, seeking a place where I could be seated and dream a little.

A raucous cackle disturbed me, catching my attention almost despite myself. Two voices were raised behind me: "Yes, yes," one was saying. "He was born under this sign, and is on his way home. Why, Zoradilla, he was born on the third of May at three in the morning..."

"Oh! Really, Lelagise," answered the other, "a curse upon the children of Saturn, this one has Jupiter in the ascendant in trine conjunction with Venus. Oh the fine young man! What natural advantages! What hopes he might entertain! What a fortune he should make! But..."

I knew the hour of my birth, and was now hearing it spelled out with the most singular precision. I turned around and stared hard at the babblers.

I saw two old gypsies not so much seated as squatting on their heels. A darker than olive complexion, eyes hollow and burning, sunken mouths, sharp, outsize noses which curved down from the tops of their heads to touch their chins; scraps of material, once striped blue and white, wound around half-bald skulls, fell like scarves around their shoulders, partially covering their nakedness; in a word, creatures almost as revolting as they were absurd.

I approached them: "Were you talking of me, ladies?" I asked them, seeing that they were continuing to stare at me and make signs.

"So you were listening, senor caballero?"

"Possibly," I answered; "and who instructed you so accurately as to the hour of my birth?"

"There is plenty more we could tell you, oh fortunate young man; but you must begin by crossing our palms."

"That need be no obstacle," I replied, and promptly gave them a doubloon.

"There you are, Zoradilla," said the older one, "see how noble he is, how he is made to enjoy all the riches for which he is destined. Come pluck your guitar and follow me," and she sang the following:
"Spain it was who gave you birth;
Parthenope nurtured you.
Master you could be of earth;
If you wanted, you could be
Darling of the Heavens, too.
The happiness foretold for you
Is fleeting, and could slip away.
You hold it at your finger tips:
If you are wise, you will obey:
Seize it unhesitatingly.
What is this object lovable
Which has submitted to your power?
Is it..."

The old women were getting into their stride. I listened eagerly, but now Biondetta came running up, having left the dance, and pulled me by the sleeve, obliging me to move away.

"Why did you leave me, Alvaro? What are you doing here?"

"I was listening," I answered...

"What?" said she, dragging me with her, "you were

94

listening to those old monsters?"

"In truth, my dear Biondetta, they are singular creatures; they know more than they are given credit for; they were telling me..."

"Oh yes," replied she scornfully, "they were acting their part and telling you your future; and you would believe them? With all your intelligence, you have the simplicity of a child. And those are the creatures who are preventing you from devoting yourself to me?"

"On the contrary, my dear Biondetta, they were about to speak to me of you."

"Speak of me?" she retorted sharply, with something like anxiety, "what do they know of me? What did they say? What nonsense you are talking. You shall dance with me all evening to make me forget this slight."

I followed her and rejoined the circle, but without heeding what was going on around me, or what I myself was doing. I was thinking only of breaking away, to take the first opportunity of rejoining my fortune-tellers. At last I sensed a favourable moment, and seized it. In the twinkling of an eye I had flown towards my witches, found them and led them towards a little arbour which stood at the end of the farm's kitchen garden. There I begged them to tell me, in prose, without riddles and very succinctly, everything of interest they might know about me. My entreaties were powerful, for I had my hands full of gold. They were burning to speak, as I was to hear them. Soon I could no longer doubt but that they were privy to the most secret particularities of my family and, after a fashion, to my liaison with Biondetta, my fears and my hopes; I felt that I was learning a great deal and I imagined that I would learn things still more important; but our Argus was now at my heels.

Biondetta did not run towards me, she flew. I attempted to speak. "No excuses," she said, "this backsliding is unpardonable."

"Ah, but you will pardon it," I said; "I am certain, although you have prevented me from acquiring even fuller knowledge, I already know enough..."

"To commit some absurdity. Indeed I am furious, but this is no place to quarrel; if we ourselves are in danger of behaving incorrectly towards one another, we do owe due consideration to our hosts. They are about to sit down at table, and I shall be sitting beside you; this time I shall take good care that you do not escape me."

The new arrangement had us seated opposite the young couple. Both were animated by the pleasures of the day; Marcos' eyes were ablaze, and Luisia looked less timid; modesty was taking its revenge and covered her cheeks with a bright blush. The Xeres wine made the rounds of the table and seemed to have somewhat thawed its reserve: even the old people, excited by the memory of pleasures past, provoked the young folk by sallies which were garrulous rather than witty. I could take in the whole picture at a glance but I had a more moving and varied one right next to me.

Biondetta, apparently torn between passion and spite, her mouth now armed with a haughty disdain, now wreathed in smiles, sulked and pinched me until the blood ran, finally stepping gently upon my foot. In a word, her behaviour bespoke favour, reproach, chastisement and affection in turn: so that, a prey to this train of emotions, I was in an inconceivable disorder.

The newly-weds had vanished, followed by some of the

guests. We too left the table; a woman, who we knew to be the farmer's aunt, took a candlestick with a yellow wax candle and led us to a small room some twelve feet square: a bed not four feet across, a table and two chairs completed the furnishings. "Monsieur and Madame," said our guide, "this is the only apartment we can offer you." She put the candlestick on the table and left us alone.

Biondetta lowered her eyes. I turned to her: "So you told them we were married?"

"Yes," she answered, "I could not tell the truth. I have your word, you have mine. That is the main thing. Your ceremonies are precautions taken against bad faith, and I set little store by them. Besides, I had no say in the matter. However, if you do not want to share the bed which has been offered us, you will mortify me by forcing me to watch you spend the night in discomfort. I need rest, I am utterly worn out." Pronouncing these words in a most spirited tone, she stretched out on the bed with her nose turned towards the wall. "What!" I cried, "Biondetta, I have displeased you, you are truly angry! How can I make amends? I would lay down my life..."

"Alvaro," she answered without bestirring herself, "go and consult your Egyptians as to the means of re-establishing tranquillity in my heart and your own."

"What! Could my conversation with those women be the cause of your anger? Ah, surely you will forgive me, Biondetta. If you knew how their opinions tallied with your own, and how they finally convinced me not to return to the castle of Maravillas! Yes, it is done, to-morrow we leave for Rome, for Venice, for Paris, for all those places where you want me to live with you. There we shall await my family's consent..."

At these words Biondetta turned around. Her face was serious, even severe. "Do you remember what I am, Alvaro, what I expected from you, what I advised you to do? What! When, after having prudently used such enlightenment as I am endowed with, I am still unable to bring you to any kind of reason, the rule of my conduct and your own shall be based on the idle utterances of two beings, the most dangerous for us both, if not the most despicable? Of course," she cried in a transport of grief, " I have always feared men; for centuries I hesitated to make a choice, but I have made one and it is irrevocable. I am unhappy indeed!" Then she melted into tears, which she tried to conceal from me.

A prey to the most violent of passions, I fell at her knees. "Oh Biondetta," I cried, "you cannot see my heart, or you would cease to rend it!"

"You do not know me, Alvaro, and you will make me suffer cruelly before you do so. I shall strive one last time to unveil my secrets to you, and so truly to gain both your esteem and your confidence, so that I shall no longer be exposed to humiliation or danger; your pythonesses are too closely in agreement with me not to inspire rightful alarm. Who can assure me that Soberano, Bernardillo, your enemies and mine, are not hidden behind these masks? Remember Venice. Let us counter their ruses by stealth. Tomorrow I arrive at Maravillas, whence they are scheming to keep me away; I shall be greeted there by the most demeaning and overwhelming suspicion. But dona Mencia is a just and estimable woman, and your brother has a noble soul: I shall abandon myself to them. I shall be a prodigy of sweetness, obligingness, obedience, patience; I shall face all assays."

She paused for a moment. "Unhappy Sylph, must you stoop lower yet?"

She would have continued, but streaming tears denied her the use of words.

What was I to do in the face of such passion, such pain, yet such restraint and brave heroic mettle? I sat down beside her and tried to calm her with caresses; at first I was repulsed, but soon I felt resistance slacken, though mine was not the merit: she was breathing with difficulty, her eyes were half-closed, her body moved convulsively, a suspect coldness had spread over her skin, her pulse was scarcely beating and her body would have seemed entirely lifeless had her tears not been flowing with unabated abundance.

Oh the power of tears, perhaps the most powerful of all love's weapons! Distrust, vows, resolutions, all were forgotten. Wishing to stem this precious dew, I drew too near to that mouth whose freshness held all the sweet scent of the rose; and even had I wished to take my distance, her arms, whose whiteness, softness and shapeliness I could never describe, were bonds whose hold I could not bear to lose...

"Oh my Alvaro," cried Biondetta, "I have triumphed; I am the happiest of beings!"

I did not have the strength to speak; I felt an extraordinary confusion, indeed I was ashamed, paralysed. She leapt out of the bed and was at my knees, removing my shoes. "What! Dear Biondetta," I cried, "why, I am unworthy..."

"Do not be harsh," she answered, "I served you while you were merely my tyrant, so let me at least serve my lover."

I was delivered of my garments; my hair was neatly gathered into a net she had found in her pocket. Her strength, her energy, her skill had surmounted the obstacles I had tried to put in their way. She executed her simple night toilette with the same promptitude, blew out the candle by which the room was lit, and quickly drew the curtains.

Then, in a voice whose sweetness would have dulled the most delicious of airs: "Have I," she asked, "made my Alvaro happy, as he has made me? No, no: this joy is mine alone; yet he must have it also. I shall intoxicate him with delights, I shall fill him with knowledge; I shall raise him to the heights of greatness. Do you, dear heart, wish to be the most privileged creature and, together with me, to submit men, the elements and all nature to your power?"

"Oh my dear Biondetta," I said, though making some effort to control myself, "you alone suffice: you fulfill all my heart's desires..."

"No, no," she retorted sharply, "Biondetta must not suffice. That is not my name: you gave it to me, and I bore it with pleasure. But you must know who I am ... I am the Devil, my dear Alvaro, the Devil ....."

By pronouncing this word in a tone of bewitching sweetness, she hermetically sealed the utterance of the answer I would have liked to have made. As soon as I could break the silence: "My dear Biondetta, or whoever you are," I said, "desist from pronouncing that fatal word and reminding me of an error long since forsworn."

"No, my dear Alvaro, it was not an error; it is what I wanted you to believe, my dear little man. I had to deceive you in order to bring you to reason. Your kind is resistant to the truth: it is only by blinding you that one can make you happy. Ah! You shall be very happy if you so desire! I intend to gratify you wholly. You will already agree that I am not as black as I am painted."

This badinage completed my confusion. I refused to be drawn in, and the drunkenness of my senses abetted my intentional abstraction.

"So, answer me," she said.

"What should I say?"

"Cruel man, put your hand on this heart that adores you; and may your heart be kindled, if this be possible, by even the faintest of the emotions so alive in my own. Let a spark of this precious flame, which has set my veins ablaze, flow through your own; soften, if you can, the sound of that voice made to inspire love, and which you use so often to alarm my timid soul; lastly, say to me, if you can, with feelings as tender as mine for you: my dear Beelzebub, I adore you..."

At that name, so tenderly pronounced, a mortal fear gripped me; astonishment and stupor overcame my soul and I would have believed it dead had not the muted voice of remorse called to me from the depths of my heart. My senses were in turmoil all the more violent for being inaccessible to reason. I was defenceless in the face of my enemy: he seized his advantage and I was wholly at his mercy.

He gave me no time to regain my composure, to reflect on the transgression of which he was indeed the author rather than the accomplice.

"The die is cast," he told me, without noticeably altering the tone to which he had accustomed me. "You sought me out. I followed you, served you, obliged you; in the end I did as you wished. I wanted to possess you and my success required you to give yourself to me freely. I may owe your first compliance to some degree of artifice; but soon afterwards I revealed myself to you: you knew who you were yielding to, and you cannot presume ignorance. Now, Alvaro, our bond is indissoluble; but to cement our association, it is important that we know each other better. And because I know you so well already, to render us equal, I must show myself to you in my true colours."

I was not given time to reflect upon this singular harangue: a sharp whistle blast sounded at my side. Instantly the surrounding darkness was dissipated and the cornice above the panelling was entirely covered with huge snails: their horns, which they moved briskly to and fro, had become jets of phosphorescent light, whose brightness was intensified by their movement and their forward thrust. Almost dazzled by this sudden illumination, I cast my eyes to my side: instead of a ravishing presence, what do I see? Oh heavens! It was the frightful camel's head. In a voice of thunder, it articulated that hollow *Che vuoi?* which had so terrified me in the grotto, then uttered a burst of human laughter more frightful still and stuck out an enormous tongue.

I rushed headlong to hide under the bed, eyes tight shut, face downwards. My heart was beating with alarming force; I gasped for breath.

How long I remained in this unaccountable situation I cannot say, but at last I felt myself being tugged by the arm; my fear increased and, forced to open my eyes, I was dazzled by a bright light.

It was not coming from the snails. They had vanished from the cornice, but the sunlight was falling straight on to my face. Again I was being pulled by the arm, and again. I recognized Marcos. "Senor caballero," said he, "at what hour were you thinking of leaving? If you want to reach Maravillas to-day you have no time to lose, it is almost mid-day."

I said nothing and he peered at me: "Senor? You slept in your bed fully dressed? You slept for fourteen hours without waking? You must have been in great need of rest. Madame sensed as much, and it was no doubt out of fear of disturbing you that she spent the night with one of my aunts. But she has outdone you in diligence: at her orders, your carriage was repaired this morning, and it is ready for your departure. As for Madame, you will not find her here: we gave her a good mule and she has gone on ahead, wanting to take advantage of the cool of the morning; she should be waiting for you in the first village you reach en route."

Marcos went out. Mechanically I rubbed my eyes and ran my hand over my head to find the net which should have held my hair. But my head was bare and my hair in disarray. Am I asleep? I asked myself. Could I be fortunate enough for all this to have been a dream? She blew out the light, I saw her do it ... There it is...

Marcos returned. "If you wish to dine, senor caballero, a meal is ready. Your carriage is harnessed..."

I climbed down from the bed but could barely stand upright, my knees buckling beneath me. I agreed to take some nourishment but found I could not eat. Then, when I wished to thank the farmer and make good the expense to which I had put him to, he refused.

"Madame has rewarded us, and more than nobly," he told me, "you and I, senor caballero, have good wives."
Thereupon, without any reply, I climbed into my chaise

103

and drove off.

I shall not depict my state of mental confusion: it was such that the idea of the danger in which I must surely find my mother was present only vaguely. Eyes glazed, mouth agape, I was less man than automaton.

My driver awoke me. "Senor caballero, we are to find Madame in this village."

I did not answer him. We drove through a straggling village; at each house he enquired whether a young woman had been seen passing by in such and such a carriage. He was told that she had not stopped. He turned around as though wishing to scan my face for disquiet. If he knew no more than I did, I must have seemed much troubled.

Now we were out of the village, and I was beginning to delude myself that the current object of my heart had taken his distance, at least for the moment. Ah! If only I could reach Maravillas, fall at dona Mencia's knees, I said to myself, if only I could put myself under the protection of my estimable mother, would these persistent ghosts and monsters dare to violate that refuge? There, amidst nature, I should again discover the wholesome principles from which I had strayed, and would use them as a breast-plate against them.

But what if the sorrow brought upon her by my misconduct had hastened the loss of my guardian angel? Oh, then I would wish to go on living only to expiate and to repent. I would bury myself in a monastery ... But even there, who would rid me of the phantoms engendered in my brain? Let us take the ecclesiastical estate, I told myself: fair sex, I must renounce you, for a fiend has donned all the graces I adored...

In the midst of these reflections, which absorbed all my attention, the carriage entered the great courtyard of the castle, and I heard a voice saying: "It is Alvaro! My son!" I raised my eyes and recognised my mother on the balcony of her apartment.

My joy and my relief were unconfined, my soul seemed born anew. I rushed forward to fly into her waiting arms. "Ah", I cried, my eyes bathed in tears, my voice shaken with sobs," ah, mother! So I am not your murderer? Would you recognize me as your son? Ah mother, you embrace me..."

My passions, and the vehemence of my actions, had so twisted my features and altered the sound of my voice, that dona Mencia seemed disturbed. Kindly she bid me rise, embraced me again, obliged me to be seated. I wanted to talk, but could not; I seized her hands, bathing them in tears and covering them with the most impassioned caresses.

Dona Mencia considered me in astonishment: something extraordinary must have befallen me, she concluded, and even feared some derangement to my reason. Her concern, her curiosity, her goodness and her tenderness were manifest in her looks as in her deeds, as she providently assembled before me all that could soothe the needs of a traveller wearied by a long and painful journey.

The servants hastened to attend to me, and I took a sip of refreshment in an attempt at politeness, my distracted glances seeking out my brother; alarmed at not seeing him, "Madame," I enquired, "where is the estimable don Juan?"

"He will be very glad to know that you are here, because he wrote requesting your return; but as his letter, written from Madrid, would have left only a few days ago, we were not expecting you so soon. You are a colonel in his former regiment and the king has just appointed him to a vice-royalty in the Indies."

"Heavens!" I cried, "Could everything in my dreadful dream be entirely untrue? It is impossible..."

"What is this dream of which you speak?"

"The longest, the most astonishing, the most frightful imaginable." Then, overcoming my pride and shame, I gave her a detailed account of what had happened to me since I had entered the grotto at Portici, until the happy moment when I had fallen at her knees.

This estimable woman heard me with extraordinary attentiveness, patience and goodness. As I well knew the extent of my fault, she saw that it was needless to magnify it.

"My dear son, you have pursued a lie and it has engulfed you. The news of my indisposition and the anger of your elder brother are sufficient proof of this. Berthe, whom you thought you spoke to, has been confined to her bed for some time. I never dreamed of sending you 200 sequins in addition to your allowance. I would have feared giving encouragement to your disorderly life, or plunging you into ill-conceived liberality. The honest squire Pimientos died eight months ago. And of the eighteen hundred villages in all Spain over which the duke of Medina-Sidonia is Lord, there is not an inch of his land at the place you mention. I know it well; you must have dreamed that farm and all its inhabitants."

"Ah, Madame," I replied, "the muleteer who brought me here saw it as I did. He danced at the wedding."

My mother ordered the muleteer to be brought forward,

but he had unharnessed the carriage on arriving , without asking for his wages.

This precipitate departure, which left no traces, threw my mother into some suspicion. "Nugnes," said she to a page who was walking through the apartment, "go and tell the venerable don Quebracuernos that my son Alvaro and I are awaiting him."

"He is a doctor from Salamanca," she continued; "he has my trust, and deserves it; you too may place your trust in him. The end of your dream has one peculiarity which confounds me; don Quebracuernos knows these mysteries and will cast light upon them better than I".

The venerable doctor did not keep us waiting. Even before he spoke, the very gravity of his demeanour was imposing. My mother bade me give a sincere account of my blunders and their consequences and he heard me out, his attention mingled with astonishment.

When I had finished, after a pause for considered thought, he spoke as follows:

"Undoubtedly, senor Alvaro, you have just escaped the greatest peril to which a man can be exposed through faults of his own making. You provoked the evil spirit and, through a series of needless acts, you furnished him with all the guises he needed to ruin and deceive you. Your adventure is truly extraordinary; I have read nothing comparable in Bodin's *Démonomanie* or Bekker's *Monde Enchanté*. And it must be admitted that, since the time of those great writers, our enemy has become prodigiously sophisticated in his strategies, exploiting ruses which men of our age deploy for their mutual corruption. He copies nature faithfully and effectively; he makes use of gracious talents, he arranges cunningly conceived gatherings and makes passions speak out in their most seductive tongue; in some ways he even imitates virtue. For me, your tale is very revealing and throws light upon many current happenings. I see clearly many grottoes more dangerous than that of Portici, and a multitude of souls obsessed who, unfortunately, do not see themselves as such. As for yourself, by taking wise precautions for the present and the future, I believe you will be entirely delivered. Your enemy has withdrawn, so much is clear. He seduced you, it is true, but he did not succeed in corrupting you; your will power and your remorse have preserved you, together with the supernal aid you have received; thus his alleged triumph and your defeat were for him and for you but an illusion, from which your repentance will wash you clean. As for him, his portion was an enforced retreat; yet one cannot but marvel at how shrewdly he covered it and, in departing, left your spirit troubled, and secret intelligences in your heart to enable him to renew the attack, should you ever offer him the opportunity. Having beguiled you, he then had to appear to you in all his deformity, and acted like a slave premeditating his revolt; he does not wish to leave you any discernible and clear image of himself, so he mingles the grotesque and the awesome, the absurdity of his luminous snails with the alarming vision of his horrible head, in a word the lie and the truth, dream and reality; thus your confused spirit can no longer make distinctions, and may believe that the vision which has beset you is rather a dream occasioned by the vapours of your brain than the effect of his evil-doing. But he has subtly preserved for you the idea of a pleasing phantom, the very one he long used to lead you astray. He will put her in your way if you let him do so. Yet I do not think the barrier of the cloister, or of our estate, is the one you should raise against him. Your vocation is not sufficiently pondered; people who have learned from experience are needed in the world. Believe me, you must form legitimate bonds with a person of the fair sex; let your estimable mother preside over your choice; and even should the one she has chosen have talents and charms divine, never would you be tempted to take her for the Devil."

Dedalus is the U.K.'s leading publisher of fantastic and decadent fiction, titles currently available include:

The Golem - Gustav Meyrink £6.99

The Angel of The West Window - Gustav Meyrink £8.99

Undine - Fouque £5.99

The Devil in Love - Jacques Cazotte £5.99

Les Diaboliques - Barbey D'Aurevilly £5.99

En Route - J.K. Huysmans £6.95

The Cathedral - J.K. Huysmans £6.95

Torture Garden - Octave Mirbeau £6.99

The Child of Pleasure - D'Annunzio £7.99

The Triumph of Death - D'Annunzio £6.99

The Dedalus Book of Decadence (Moral Ruins) - editor Brian Stableford £7.99

Tales From The Saragossa Manuscript - Potocki £5.99

The Wandering Jew - Eugene Sue £9.99

Tales of The Wandering Jew - Editor Brian Stableford £8.99

Micromegas - Voltaire £4.95

The Red Laugh - Leonid Andreyev £4 .95

Seraphita - Balzac £6.99

The Quest of The Absolute - Balzac £4.95

The Phantom of The Opera - Leroux £6.99

The Arabian Nightmare - Robert Irwin £5.95

The Revenants - Geoffrey Farrington £3.95

The Acts of The Apostates - Geoffrey Farrington £6.99

These titles can be ordered from all good local bookshops or directly from
Cash Sales, Dedalus Ltd, Langford Lodge, St Judiths Lane, Sawtry, Cambs, PE17 5XE.
Please send a cheque to the value of the remittance adding 75p for the first title, thereafter 50p to a maximum of £3.00 pp.